THE KINGDOM'S TREASURES

BOOK TEN

JP ROSSELLE

TABLE OF CONTENTS

CHAPTER I

MONTIBELLI'S WILL

I HAD NOT MET THE SHAH nor any of the Shah's family. It was only by chance that my course had run into Montibelli. At that time, several shipping containers were being shipped to the Sandinistas down in Nicaragua. Those Containers were being shipped out of the Port of New Orleans. If most of the containers hadn't been overweight, they would have been shipped out as planed. The overweight problem was then compounded by the fact that the shipping line couldn't contact the shipper to discuss the overweight issue. Without being able to contact the shipper, the shipping line then contacted the container leasing company that owned the containers. The container leasing company then discovered that their New York office had been tricked into dispatching empty containers that they thought were for one of their good customers. The trouble was, their customer knew nothing of the pick up of the 17 empty containers, nor did they request the equipment.

Here's where I got involved. I was called by the container leasing company, they requesting me to urgently fly to New Orleans and recover their containers. At that point, no one knew that the overweight containers were loaded with a decommissioned Howitzer factory. I did what my customer had requested; I recovered the 17 containers, but also the cannon factory that was packed into the containers.

Montibelli soon appeared wanting his property back.

Eventually, Montibelli did get his cargo back; it was reloaded and shipped to Iran. Iran at the time was at war with Iraq. Montibelli was also known to my old friend Bob and the Colonel. Turned out the the Colonel was looking for revenue to assist the Contras in Nicaragua. At the time, Congress had cut off funding for the Contras that were resisting the Sandinistas.

Montibelli had been a Iranian General for the Shah. Soon after the Shah's death, Montibelli became one of the world's largest international arms dealers. Somehow along the way, Montibelli and I became friends.

Today my Attorney Roy would be showing up here in Nassau. Roy was bringing with him Montibelli's last will and testimony.

Montibelli had died months ago in the Times Square attack. I wasn't in any hurry to see his will. Now, Roy, he had some urgency as he felt that somehow someone was looking for information that the will may hold. Roy was afraid that whoever wanted the will would hurt him or his family to get it.

Roy arrived in Nassau via commercial airlines in the company of Big Ted and Steve. If you don't remember, Big Ted and Steve were members of the Miami Metro Police Department. It had been some years since I had seen Steve, seemed the family life had taken hold. Big Ted was the same Metro Detective not afraid to stick his neck out.

The old Hurricane house in downtown Nassau would be our today's meeting place. Roy asked that it only be the two of us that read the will.

The words of Montibelli's will were short. It read that "all his worldly possessions were to go to his only friend," myself. Then there was a long list of assets that included bank accounts plus stocks and bonds. All neatly logged with a bottom line with each item. In the list of assets were names and contact information. With each name wasn't their monetary value, but their value just the same. On the sixth page he noted that he had left me my greatest adventure of all. Montibelli stated it was the Shah's touchable assets that the Shah couldn't have taken with him when he had left Iran. These items were smuggled out of Iran. "Yes", Montibelli wrote " all the families gold and jewelry except the Crown Jewels." "The location of the Shah's Treasure is on a map that is already in your possession," he wrote. "You think you are the only one that knows about this safe, but you are wrong," he wrote. "I know how you like puzzles so I also left you one that I believe we could have together solved, it was not to be", "Be careful what you wish for, it's all about the women, your friend Montibelli." Roy looked at me and said he didn't want to know.

It was strange, I knew exactly the safe Montibelli was talking about. I didn't understand how he could have known or ever been there. Carson wouldn't have told anyone but me. I hadn't been there in years. This safe was, of course the safe in Carson's house garage floor drain.

Roy would then be on his way, straight back to the airport then flying back home to Miami. Roy had flown in to Nassau carrying only a black briefcase. Roy took nothing with him on his travel back to Miami to show whoever may have been watching him that he no longer had what they were looking for. They were, of course, watching. Ted said he would call once Roy was safely home.

Montibelli had amassed a fortune in cash and his large portfolio included only the top stocks. Of course, Montibelli had invested a large sum in IBM and G.D. There was one stock's name that stuck out like a sore thumb. The stocks name was, "Summa Technolgiae", the name was Latin, my English interpretation was "artificial intelligence." The reason I knew the Latin translation was that the only other time I had seen that same name was in looking at the list of stocks that Pearl had. The company appeared to be privately held and was the only item on Montibelli's list that didn't state a worth in dollars and cents. Funny, I had in my hands reach a new cash amount of over 239 million plus stocks worth well over another 100 million, plus a treasure map that should have had me foaming at the mouth, yet the thing that had my mind spinning was this one stock that both Pearl and Montibelli shared.

Pearl's explanation of the stock was that long ago, her mother's brother had left the group to live within what her mother called the rat race. The rat race was of course us humans. Pearl said she had never met her uncle. When I asked Eorum and Ant, Ant said it was before his time; Eorum said he was a small boy of about eight years old when Victoria's brother left the group. It was sometime after Pearl's Grandfather, the captain, was killed in the big channel, Eorum said. Victoria's brother had decided to venture out on his own. Eorum had said that it was years later when he and Victoria had gone to search for Victoria's husband, that Victoria had contacted her brother for his help with her husband's location. Eorum said that even then he himself didn't actually see the brother. The stocks that Pearl's mother had left her were from part of the envelope that Victoria had brought down with her from the brother's large office building. Eorum said he wasn't allowed up, the security was tight. I had asked Eorum if he remembered the sign on the building? Eorum said it was easy to remember; it was IBM. My mind raced when he told me.

Before I knew it, I was at the end of the main Nassau dock, standing daydreaming about the past. It was here on this very spot that Michelle and I had become partners. That was 21 years ago;

Michelle's ashes were cast over at the location of the first treasure. Cat's ashes were put here into the outgoing tied. I was brought back by a loud whistle, I turned and saw Lori and June walking my way. Before they reached me June said she was looking for a boyfriend. Lori came and kissed me and said it was for real. June then said, my turn little sister and said she was taught to kiss by an expert. As the three of us started to walk back to the main gate, I glanced around; for a moment, I thought I saw Michelle. I blinked and she was gone.

Before leaving the dock, I stuck my head into the Bar and inquired about Willy. The young man said that Willy hadn't been in for days. We would walk to Willy's house; we found him sitting on his porch. He didn't meet us half way up to his home's walkway. He looked tired; Willy smiled with pride and thanked us for stopping by. Willy said he was on the porch waiting for his dinner to be delivered by Otis. Willy said that Otis still brought him either a large grouper or two good size crawfish. Willy looked at the girls, Lori with another big belly and June; he said things hadn't changed much. Looking at me, Willy said only our ages. Willy then announced what he thought was my first gray hair. I looked at Willy and said, at least I still had some. Willy and I laughed.

Although Montibelli had handed me just what I was looking for, I had no one to go adventure hunting with. My friends either had died or got tied up with women that had them by the balls. Of course someone looking from the outside might have thought the same of me. I should have been content, but I was not.

Big Ted called that night and said that Roy had made it home. Ted said that there were at least two men that had followed Roy to Nassau. Only one had left the Island. Ted said the man who stayed was not the typical roughneck but a wealthy businessman without a criminal background. Ted said that Steve had stayed in Nassau to meet with my security there, to pass the wand. Ted said that Steve had caught the last night's flight out. Ted said they would keep track of the man that had returned to the mainland to see where he lead them. Ted said he had contacted Jerry to send a team to relieve his men.

I checked the computer, these days the computer netted very little activity. Jerry had confirmed that he was on both men's backgrounds; Jerry said he would put a tail on the man that came back to Miami on the same plane as Roy and Ted.

By morning I had more news, the man in Miami was found dead in his Four Ambassadors hotel room. The Miami police said it looked to have been some overdose of medication. Ted had been notified and would assist Jerry's man in the follow-up. Thus far, it looked like the dead man was a John Doe; his passport and other ID were false. Our Nassau visitor's name was Rodgers; he was a well-known aviation engineer designer that had worked on the original Apollo Moon mission. Since then, he was well known for his many failed attempts to build and fly what many said was a spacecraft that could take off from the earth, enter the atmosphere and return to earth. Winston Churchill had described success as one that walked in one failure after another failure ending with the same enthusiasm.

I would find myself at Mr. Rodgers's boarding house door that same morning.

Mr. Rodgers was dressed and ready to receive me. Mr. Rodgers apologized for how we were meeting. As we walked toward the docks, Mr. Rodgers told me how he had met the General. Rodgers was of course referring to Montibelli.

Rodgers said he was working on one of his projects and Montibelli had appeared out of the blue. Rodgers said he was in desperate need of money and had sold the General his technology stocks. Mr. Rodgers said that he had heard that the General had been killed at the Time Square shootings and thought that there could be the chance to buy his stocks back. Mr. Rodger said the stocks were worthless. I asked, if worthless then why follow my attorney here, why want the stocks back. Mr. Rodgers said that he had worked with a man at IBM that had started a company in his house garage. The man, Mr. Rodgers said was a genius. Maximus, Rodgers said, had scribbled a design for what I could only say was a flying machine. No, he then said, it was a spaceship. In 1960, Maximus offered Rodgers a job. I assisted Maximus in moving from his garage, purchasing an old abandoned warehouse. There, Mr. Rodgers said we worked nights and our days off from IBM. We were building what Maximus called the ship. The ship looked like what many people would have said was a flying saucer. Maximus had made a material that was a mixture of metal and fiberglass. The material was lightweight but stronger than steel. The engine was electric, powered by a large battery. It wasn't long after that Maximus was impressed by Kennedy's moon speech. Somehow Maximus got to meet Kennedy's brother Robert then the President himself. Just two months after Maximum had met with the President, Kennedy was assassinated. The very next day our flying machine was stolen, and the warehouse was burned to the ground. Maximus then went to work for NASA. Maximus had dragged me along; we were there until Apollo 11 successfully returned to earth. Then abruptly, Maximus went back to work at IBM again, taking me with him. In the early 1970s Maximus disappeared. Rodgers said it was a short time later that he received the stocks in the mail. Rodgers said there was no return address.

It was early in 1980 when Montibelli appeared, on the tract of Maximus. Rodger said after Maximus disappeared, other than receiving the stocks he never saw or heard from Maximus again. When Montibelli showed, I needed the money; Montibelli wanted the stocks.

Rodger continued saying that late last year, IBM contacted him looking for Maximus; IBM implied that their central computer system might have been implanted with some artificial intelligence. Computers first started communicating, first with each other, then sending their own messages. Computers rented space, ordered parts and material, hired labor, set up manufacturing and boom. A new company was set up and running. Rodger said all this was financed and paid for from a foreign bank account with the code name, you guessed it, Summa Technolgiae. Rodgers said that IBM wasn't upset; they wanted in. IBM said whatever had been placed into their computers had just like that disappeared.

Rodgers said he thought there was more to it.

Rodgers said, just think if someone really did control our computers, even what if the computers were in control. Rodgers said the stocks were only paper if a working company didn't exist. What would you do with the stock I asked? No I thought, there was something missing. Something that Rodgers wasn't telling me.

I had an idea, I walked Rodgers back to the boarding house and told him that I would do some investigating and for him to sit tight. I also mentioned that he wasn't the only man on the plane that had followed Roy; the other man is now dead. I told him I would be leaving a security detail to watch over him.

My thought was to go back home and get into the computer and connect with TESS.

When arriving home, there had been a few calls from Big Ted and Jerry. I contacted Jerry first; Jerry said that there could have been a third person of interest on the plane that had come in with Roy. Jerry said that they had run a list of the passengers and one more name came up; it was a Russian operative. Jerry thought KBG. Jerry said that Big Ted now had the ID of the dead man, that man Jerry said was an Iranian operative. Jerry said we must have something they want. I thought, the Iranians might want the treasure and the Russians the technology.

I then called Ted; he confirmed the dead man's identity and said the accidental death would now be moved to homicide.

Just as soon as I could, I would get into the computer. I say that as my office door had several children standing in my doorway. Then the boss showed up. No, not Lori and not June; it was Betty. You'd know you ain't supposed to be in there working with the door shut, Betty said. Yous already in a heap of trouble, Betty said. Then it hit me; today was Lori's doctor's appointment in Miami. It turned out that June had gone with Lori taking the Leer and with them Pearl too. I looked at my watch and saw that I had missed the appointment.

The computer was now up and waiting; it had made contact with the TESS computer in Paix that was aboard the C-130 parked there. I typed in, "good evening TESS," at first there was no reply, then, "Good evening, Captain, we have missed you." I then typed in, "is Maximus there?" TESS waited and then answered, "General Maximus died more than 2,000 years ago". "We fought along his side until the Romans lost there way." I realized that TESS had carefully answered my question without giving me the answer; I believed it knew whom I was looking for. Please pass the message to Maximus that I now have control of 75% of his company's stocks, and I'd like to meet with him. TESS replied, "message received."

My mind raced; could it be that Maximus had built a computer system that had a thinking process of its own? Why did it seem so odd? We had seen where TESS had made some of its own decisions. I thought about it, maybe the computer or computers would have the personality of the inventor. If so, then maybe I should introduce Pearl to TESS.

Victoria, if she would have lived, would have been about 70; if Maximus was an older brother, then he could be in his 70s. My dad was now 65 and he still thinks he can whip me. This all still left me with just one thing. How was I going to get loose and with whom. Lori was now pregnant with our second, June, she already had her hands full. Neither woman was going to let me disappear without a fight.

The woman folk came home just after dark. Lori said she and our daughter were doing fine; yes, Lori said, it is going to be a girl! We will have our Joe-Anne, Lori said with a smile. Lori said her due date would put Joe-Anne as a Leo, being born sometime during mid-August. Ant and Eorum were busy moving the purchases as the girls had also gone shopping. Ant had traveled with Pearl while Eorum had spent the day with Willy. I was sure Willy had given Eorum an ear full. June said that Cindy and Jack were also in Miami shopping, both had flown in with Madelyn and Charles. Cindy and Jack had purchased one of the houses Charles and I had purchased on Eleuthera and fixed up. Jack now had the Cessna that I had loaned to Richard, the Government had finally replaced the one that Richard, and I had been downed in by the Sandinistas. June said that Cindy said she was worried about Jack, Jack; Cindy noted Jack wasn't eating or sleeping very well. Lori added that Jack had the Captain syndrome. It just slipped out, "boredom," I said; it could be he's bored. Betty jumped into the conversation and said, yeah, but he doesn't have two wives and nine children to keep him busy and don't you forget you have your tenth child and your first grandchild on the way! Betty then said looking at Lori, you best keep this man away from Mr. Jack, thems two together spells nothing but trouble!

Yes, there were some laughs, but mine wasn't one of them.

The next day I again passed by the boarding house to visit with Rodgers. To my surprise, during the night, he had checked out and gotten a flight back to Miami. I put in a call for Big Ted, and Ted said that one of Jerry's men had eyes on Rodgers from Miami International. Jerry would report that night that we were not the only ones watching Rodgers as our Uncle Sam was also watching.

It would be more than two weeks before I got the chance to have Pearl sit at the computer with me. I though I was was smarter than she was but I was wrong. Pearl asked what I wanted to know from TESS? I was straight with her, I'm looking for your uncle Maximus. Pearl looked at me and asked if I had proof that he was still alive? I said I didn't know and then told her what I thought and why I was looking for him. Pearl said that Victoria never talked about her brother. I said, your mother, Pearl said that Lori was her mother. Pearl then paused and said Lori is my mother, my sister, and my best friend. Pearl then sat at the keyboard and started typing. I couldn't read what she was writing because Pearl wrote in Latin. Almost as fast as she wrote, TESS responded. It all made no since to me. TESS then wrote "Commander, Maximus is not available at the moment, out fishing I believe is the correct term." Pearl laughed at the comment, I then typed in, what happened to calling me Captain? TESS answered back, "Congratulations are in order, you have received a promotion." Pearl laughed again. Pearl then typed in, that will be all for the moment. Pearl then said that when she had seen Cindy and Jack in Miami, Jack mentioned how he missed the action and said that she had promised to take him fishing after their baby was born.

It wasn't long before Cindy and Jack came to Nassau; three days later, Cindy gave birth to a beautiful little girl named Salinas; tears came to my eyes as I was told the name.

Dan had flown in for the weekend; Maria had also flown in from Paxi.

Dan gave us some of the updates on what the Government was doing with TESS. TESS was now being tested against unmanned targets. The main problem so far, Dan said, was that TESS still considered anything that was armed as a potential threat. TESS even fired on each other. Dan said they had recently lost two C-130s to friendly fire. Both units had crashed with no loss of life.

Dan said one General had argued that he believed that I was somehow controlling TESS. The two C-130s that went down both had cut off parts of the other's tail. When I heard that, my private thought was it could be the work of Maximus.

Dan said that his job was keeping up with us, us meaning our air traffic and movements. In other words, it's a tedious job except for Jerry. Jerry is getting most of the attention Dan said. I haven't spoken to him lately, but with his new DHL cargo contract, his Crowbe connection, and the new charter service, Jerry's business has quickly grown into something for them to think about. Their worried about where his money is coming from and how easy SCS could be used into supplying a major ground movement, Dan said.

We all asked Dan about Heather? Dan said that Heather was no longer in uniform and had moved to what he thought was the CIA. Heather had now made several overnight trips that Dan wasn't in agreement with.

Dan said his level of boredom was why he was here. Dan said that they, of course, knew of the murdered Iranian in Miami and that the Iranian had just come back from a relatively short visit from Nassau. Yes he said, Mr. Rodgers was also on their list of persons of interest. Dan said that they saw no connection between the Iranian and Rodgers, but they did know you had met with Rodgers. Dan asked if there was an adventuring brewing? With none of us replying, Dan then said I'm not married to her. Jack then laughed and said, sleeping with the daughter while working for the father. Maria said, Jack's got you there. It wasn't long before Lori joined us on the porch. Lori announced that Miss Angee was on the way with some fresh crawfish and conch fritters.

We were all still sitting on the porch when two T28s buzzed us. At first, Dan looked concerned, that was until he saw Lori waving and the planes waving their wings back. It was of course Pearl and Johnny. Lori said the planes had been too big to fit under the tree but that Santa had dropped them off for Christmas. As the planes came back around both did spins for us to see. Dan asked if they had regular pilots with them? Lori said it had been like the first bike most kids got. Both came with a seasoned fighter pilot, but like the training wheels of a bicycle, they were soon left behind. Lori then mentioned that Pearl had started giving the Captain a refresher course. Dan asked if I could fly like that? I said that I had never really flown a plane by myself and still hadn't. Jack then asked if the kids might let him and I barrow them one morning. The plane buzzing had brought Cindy and June out from the house. Cindy had caught the last part that Jack had said and commented that yes, Jack needed something to keep him busy. Cindy said that Jack had been mopping around the house long enough. That to me sounded like permission. Dan then asked if he too, could get in on the flying? June then quickly added, if it's flying, then the Captain has permission, but no fishing trips. We all got her drift.

Maria didn't talk much in front of Dan nor the womenfolk; Maria stayed a day longer than Dan. Dan looked sad to go back, I thought he was looking for a permanent invite. That invite couldn't come until after the decision to leave the Pentagon and Heather.

Maria, Jack and I took several Long Beach walks, Maria had become our number one. Maria informed us where we were in Nicaragua; Joel hadn't lost a man or woman in Nicaragua in almost six months. Our people were keeping busy but without much if any resistance. Maria now was just over the 100 man-mark with all being air dropped, at one time or another, into Nicaragua's jungle for training missions. We now had a larger Air Force, buying two

Huey Helicopters to be used for rescue missions. Maria would have a small group dropped over open waters, and the Huey's would go and pick them up. We now had almost 20 retired Air Force and Navy Pilots. The Paxi chateau had once again turned into operation headquarters, and more Paxi construction was underway. We had all this going on with no clear plan for a fishing trip.

Jack and I would start seeing each other regularly. We both got plenty of hours in the T28s.

August came bringing Joe-Anne. Lori was now the proud mother of two plus Pearl. We were all one big happy family. Oh yes, I was now a grandfather. Wendy Michelle and Joe had a baby girl. They named her Catherine and would call her Cat.

CHAPTER II

PANAMA INVASION

WE HAD A GREAT THANKSGIVING, and Christmas was fast approaching. Dan showed up out of the blue.

Dan said that there was something going on that he thought would interest our group. His information was that the President had ordered to invade Panama and silence Noriega before Noriega could add to the damage of the President's standing popularity. It was Dan's idea for us to kidnap Noriega before he could be silenced.

Dan said that once Noriega was sure what were the President's intentions, to save his own life, Noriega would spill whatever beans he had. Beans such as Noriega working with the CIA under the instructions of his ex- CIA handler, our new President. Dan said he understood that he wouldn't be able to go back to the Pentagon or Heather.

We wouldn't have much time to get ready; we put together a plan as we knew what bait we would need to attract such a fish. Maria knew just the girl; it would be Carla's younger sister. Shirley had been a member of our group for almost two years. She was a young looking 18 year old, as good-looking as they get. Back when Lucy was raped and almost beaten to death by the Navy personal, Lucy's best friend Carla was the other victim that they raped and beat so badly. They had run over Carla with their car to try and hide what they had done to her. Shirley was Carla's younger sister. It wasn't Noriega that had done this terrible deed but the Sailors had been using drugs at the time. Shirley was on board with the plan.

We would also need Evette as Maria taught Shirley some Spanish, but Evette was still young and beautiful and could speak Noriega's native language.

Noriega's spent a lot of time in two local bars in a poor part of Panama City. On our second day in Panama, we made contact. As things went, Noriega traveled with a group of 6 men. Noriega and his men were taken by surprise and without a shot being fired. Shirley was armed with a small but convincing, spring field five-shot 45 semiautomatic. Her gun was now pointed at Noriega's chest. If this hadn't happened on the night of December 19th, things might not have happened as they did. Jack had been aboard our most sophisticated C-130 with the advanced radar. We were notified that U.S. ground troops stationed in Panama were on the move, plus more than 17 U.S. helicopters were headed in our direction. Jack couldn't do much with the advancing ground troops, but he did raise havoc with the airborne units. We had given Noriega a sort of sedative to calm him down. We had now moved him; we left his guards bound and gagged. We had now set up in a Catholic Church, using the bishop's office. At first Noriega seemed in denial that what we told him was happening. Once we were in the church, Jack had TESS back off, and the attack seemed to be in full gear. We had Noriega's radio, and he could hear his commanders calling for total resistance to the U.S. attack. We told Noriega that there was an order to shoot to kill for him. Once the reality set in, Noriega asked what we wanted? The story in trade for your life. We convinced him that his story and any proof he had was his only chance for him to stay alive. We started filming, he started talking. Noriega also shared the location where he kept the proof of his story. He kept repeating that he couldn't believe that he was being betrayed by those he had helped rise to power. Noriega was weary that after we had the information, we would kill him anyway. Here's where the Bishop came into play. The Bishop assured that he would personally negotiate his surrender to the attacking troops. I assured Noriega that I would retain the information, guarding it to guarantee his well-being. Via radio, Noriega cleared the way to get to the information we were looking for. Our recovery group was gone just two hours before returning with a briefcase of information and photos. Communicating through Jack, we were able to contact the Admiral and the Director. Before our first contact, we had safely dispatched our signed statement, along with our video and the all-telling briefcase. Once the call was made, it still took some time for any U.S. troops to arrive at the church; we all were long gone. Jack would once again use TESS's magic. Our ground group that was the last to leave, along with our group that had safely brought out the information, were now aboard our two copters over Costa Rica. We rendezvoused in Limon where Dan, Maria, Shirley, Evette and myself would board Jack's C-130. We were in and out of Limon before anyone even knew we had been there. The fishing trip thus far had resulted in no shots fired, and no one hurt. All were accounted for. Aboard the C-130, we again looked at some, primarily photos, checks copies, and wire transfers. The photos included many of the players but wouldn't prove much. It was the transfers that Noriega said could bring down the President. We put everything back in the briefcase, and I handed it to Maria and wrote on a yellow pad that we would make copies and store in two different places. Maria read the note and gave me the thumbs up.

Neither Jack or I had gotten permission for the trip. As we returned to Paxi, I noticed both T28s on the ground. Tommy's Leer was also there. What we had should keep Noriega alive and us out of physical harm from the current administration for quite some time. We, being Jack and myself, hoped that the girls would see our fishing trip as something good for the family. As we landed in Paxi, we could see the girls there standing near the runway. The ramp wasn't entirely down as yet, but I could see Lori running toward the ramp. It was her running part that had me smiling, smiling for the first time since the start of the trip. I jumped out on the tarmac, and we hit each other from a run. We both said we were sorry at the same time, then kissed. Lori turned, and with my hand In hers, she started heading to one of the parked T28s. You can fly this thing, she asked? I fly better than I ride a bike, I said. Yes, Lori said, your only bike was the one your father gave you for your 7th birthday. Yes, I said, and I swim better than I walk. Where we off to I asked? Eleuthera, Lori said.

It wasn't my first landing on Eleuthera; Pearl and I had used Eleuthera for my take-off and landing practices. Pearl was also giving Lori flying lessons.

It wasn't, well maybe it was; Lori and I had lost something, until that moment I saw her running to the C-130's ramp; I was anxious to get Lori into the shower. My thought until we got to the Harbor Island house was just that. We showered, napped, and found enough clothes to walk on down to the Pink Sands for some food.

It was on our way walking to the hotel that we heard the helicopters coming from the other side of the Island. The copters weren't ours and seemed to be heading to the house. As they hovered over the house, they must have seen us. I hadn't seen our security and asked if Lori had mentioned to anyone where we were going? Lori said that Cindy knew. I looked down at my new Viper radio, and its red light was blinking. As I grabbed the radio, a Black T28 flew by between us and the two copters. As the T28 zoomed by, it then made a turn to port as to come back around facing the copters. At about the same time, one of our Huey's came in and faced the two intruders. Right behind the Huey, at about 2,000 feet, one of our C-130s flew over, traveling from the west to the east. The two intruder copters then put down on the beach. As they did, several men came out from the palm trees with arms pointing their way. One copter door opened, and out stepped the Director. His hand were stretched out wide and one of our men met him face to face. During this, the T28 had come back around flying south. As the T28 passed, it waved its wings then headed almost straight up into the sky, completing a 360. A voice on the radio then said, "I bought my own Christmas present this year, how do you like it?" Before I could answer, my viper was now beeping. Sir, the Director, would like a word with you. The Director was a good 100 yards from us but I could see his jacket and his tie flapping from the copters blades still turning. "Tell him he's overdressed for dinner." With that, I saw the Director pull off his tie and take it and the jacket and give it to our man. Our man checked and radioed that he was unarmed. I said to send him on our way. As the Director walked our way, Lori squeezed my hand and said how much she loved me, our children, and the life together we all have. Lori said if I needed more adventure she would gladly accompany me to search for the Shah's treasure but please stay away from that corrupt Government. As the director walked up, I apologized as he wouldn't be having dinner with us after all. The Director said he understood and said it was him that needed to apologize for the disruption. I'll be direct he said, the President wants to know what you intend to do with the information you have? Tell the President that the information, all that I have, is safe for as long as we are left alone and Noriega is treated within the terms of his surrender. The Director then offered his congratulations on our newborn. The T28 still was making it's circle. The Director looked up and said, like father like son. Lori quickly said daughter. The Director said that she ought to enlist in the Air Force. Then he said maybe not.

I looked at the Director and asked if we were clear? He said we were. As the Director walked away, Lori thanked me. As the T28 came around one more time, at a heading that all could see, the T28 did a spin that I nor anyone that saw it would think possible. We turned and continued our walk north. Before we reached the hotel, all behind us had disappeared.

CHAPTER III

CHRISTMAS

I T WAS JUST TWO DAYS before Christmas Eve; we had big plans for Christmas; Wendy Michelle, Joe, and their daughter, my granddaughter Cat, would be visiting. Lori and I would be married for three years. Where did the time go?

Christmas would have been a joyous day. Willy had been at the house Christmas eve and had planned to be there when the children opened their presents. Angee had stopped by this morning to give him a ride. Willy had died peacefully in his sleep on Christmas Morning. We didn't tell the children; Christmas, I always said, was for the children. It was the day a great man was born, but most of our faith celebrated his birth every day.

I hadn't known until today; Angee said that her Johnny had also been born Christmas Day. Johnny would have been 36 years old. When Angee told me, I smiled and said I should have known by Johnny's all teeth smile.

The house was full of children, I counted 19, little ones under the age of 11. Seven of those are my own. With our adopted, June, Lori and I now have 11. June said that was enough children.

Christmas went fine, Pearl and Johnny showed off in Pearl's new T28 at the beachside. This plane had been built using some of

Pearl's ideas. The engine was over 1,000 horsepower and, of course, was much faster than the other two T28s that Pearl and Johnny had been flying. Pearl had me a bit concerned as to what she would buy next. Whatever she did, Johnny would be right behind her. I was good with Johnny being the co-pilot but wasn't sure Johnny could keep up with how quickly Pearl was advancing. Also, there now was the fact that the pilots of the C-130s warned and complained that they couldn't keep tabs on the new T28 because of its speed. Jack reiterated that once Pearl was 100 plus miles ahead of the C-130s, they'd have difficulty protecting her. They definitely wouldn't be able to catch her.

Maria was at the house for Christmas and brought along Shirley; I thought by what I saw that Shirley had maybe brought along Maria. Looked like Shirley had eyes on Dan. Johnny and Carolina were still going strong. Johnny's time with Pearl didn't seem to bother Carolina. Pearl either spent time in the air, on the computer, or in the shop working her ideas with Rodgers. Melody was still the fisherman of the group. Both Melody and Sam had learned to sail by taking Pram lessons at the Coconut Grove Sailing Club and certainly knew their way around the Hobie cat. Over here, they needed something smaller than the Hunter but larger than the Hobie. I thought about sailing over the Morgan but didn't want not to have presents at the sailing club in the Grove. It had been almost a year since I was in Miami. Lee and Janie, with their three little ones, had come back to Nassau for the Holidays. Diane and Marcos that were now living in Tampa, were here too with their twin boys. Jena was a no-show so far, leaving us to wonder just how she was doing with motherhood. June had mentioned that Little Joe might end up being our 12th.

We hadn't visited General Santos this past Summer so we made sure that Malcolm's group got here. Malcolm's group included his wife Mia, their daughter, Nilo, and his wife.

The children had Christmas wrapping paper everywhere; the two Haitian girls that Salinas had brought from Paxi were still with us, them hardly being able to keep up with the little ones.

The adults would have a sit-down dinner while the kids ate out by the pool. We decided we would have Willy's funeral tomorrow, Willy had said that he, too, wanted to be cremated and his ashes put into the outgoing tide from his bar's dock end. With Willy would go the many old stories he told anyone who would listen. Many of the tourists that had listened to Willy's stories either thought that he had made them up or at least the Famous Captain Jim had long ago died. Lori, said that the stories would live on; one can't walk the docks without hearing someone telling stories of The Captain and the Queen of Nassau, and, of course, then were the stories of the Famous Captain Cat. Down on the Fisherman's pier they still tell how Captain Cat saved Captain Jim's life in a bar fight. Some stories say that Captain Cat sails out there today searching for the Captain. The stories also say that when the Captain sailed off, he promised to return one day. Lori looked at me and said she wasn't sure if I had indeed returned or if I hadn't left as yet.

Diane broke the silence; she stood with her glass in hand and said, "to the Captain." All stood saying here here. I stood and said, "here's to Willy; they'll be forever hearing his stories up there."

With Willy's funeral came Bob's first visit to the Island in more than a year.

I had met Bob and Willy on that same summer day. Yes, it was Rusty's and my first day in Nassau some 24 years ago; Willy was the bartender, and Bob was in his safari uniform with a tigress on each arm; we six were the only ones in the City Dock Bar that day.

Bob and Angee cried at the dock as we poured Willy's ashes into the outgoing tide. Angee didn't for one minute let go of Bob's arm.

Bob said he no longer drank hard liquor, but in Willy's house, we found a bottle of 24-year-old scotch that I felt Willy had been saving for a special occasion. Bob stopped by the Hill Top house to see the family then left back to Miami on the evening flight.

New Year's Eve would be on us; that day, I again visited the graves of Deanna and Salinas. I didn't celebrate the new year coming in. It was just a year ago when the Times Square attack had taken place. Montibelli and others lost their lives that night. Two of the men that had planned and ordered the attack were still out there. I say two because the Director had sent word that they had new information that connected the Drug Lord Escobar.

We had information that Escobar was starting to feel the pressure and had talked with the Colombian President about a surrender that included the promise that he would not be deported. I was told that even a special jail was being built for Escobar that could be defended from a foreign Government or a competitor's air attack. I heard it would be more like a five-star hotel than a prison. The Russian on the other hand, we heard was much closer to us. General Micoski was said to have visited Robert Vesco's house in Cuba but was denied being protected by the Castros. General Micoski was now said to be in Nicaragua. I had once met Vesco in Nassau; at that time, his yacht was docked at the Nassau City docks. It was then in the late '70s that Vesco was said to be marketing Paradise Island for sale.

Maria was aware of the Russian General's presents in Nicaragua; however, even though we were looking, we hadn't yet located him. For the time being, Escobar might be out of reach, but if the General would stay put for a short time, I felt we could get at him.

I would need to visit Carson's old house for the treasure map, but that could be a security risk for Lee's family, who was staying there.

The American Government now had two wrecked Vehicles, the one that was highly radioactive and was at Homestead and the other in New Mexico in their secret area 51. Lee was still working the Homestead construction contract. Lee and family were living in Carson's house until this June when the project would be completed. We weren't ready to go treasure hunting, although I knew the longer we waited, the more chance someone other than us might find it. I was sure there were many people looking, to include the Shah's oldest son, the Iranian Government and anyone else that might know of the treasure. It was a Monday morning; Lee's construction company would be closed the rest of the week with Lee and family on the Island until this Friday.

Jack and I would fly over and land at the Tamiami Airport in Miami. We would have Dan in the C-130 watching over us, Dan making sure not to travel into the U.S. airspace. Jack and I would fly one of the original T28s keeping it below the radar. I remembered that in 1969 a Cuban defector had flown his MiG from Cuba to Homestead Air Force Base without being detected by radar. As things sometime go, the Cuban Captain that had flown that MiG had afterward worked in our first container yard as a welded. I had heard his story several times.

In our T28, we would fly across the Gulf Stream only high enough to miss the swells; we crossed through the Sand's Cut channel, then on to South Miami, landing at the Tamiami Airport training strip.

Not everyone in our group knew of the Montibelli treasure map, yes I had mentioned it to Jack, and of course, Lori and June knew. I had, until reading Montibelli's will, thought I was the only living soul that knew about Carson's garage floor safe. If the map were in Carson's garage safe, then maybe, just maybe, Montibelli would have a note spilling the beans on just how he found the safe.

Jack told the airport staff at Tamiami that we had flown out of a privet airstrip in Naples and gotten lost. The airport staff was more interested in the T28 than they were us. We told the airport staff that we would catch a bite of lunch and be back to fly back home.

We caught a cab and headed to Carson's old house. I guess I was lucky that Jack was along; neither of the house guards acted as if they knew me, they did know Jack, and we were permitted inside. Wouldn't you know it the old Mercedes was on the wrong side of the garage. Of course, the car didn't start; we must have looked like fools, opening the garage door, then pushing that car out of the garage, and then back in on the other side. I hadn't planned to empty the safe but by making the car move, then closing the garage door. Anyone seeing this could or would figure it out. Jack was surprised at the steps it took to open the safe. First, it was the removal of the steering wheel of the Mercedes, then adding an extension to the steering wheel, then putting the extension into the drain, and then turning the wheel as the block of cement rose until I could pull out the box. I had brought along a briefcase and emptied the boxes contents, Including Carson's Gold Cup 45, into the case. We then returned the empty box and began turning the steering wheel back to lower the box back into the cement hole. I had to be sure that the cement was positioned just right to match the drain hole. We then got the sealant that was there in a cabinet and resealed the cement. A bag of drying powder was still there; I used it to dust the top of the cement. I returned the extension and steering wheel, and we were done. We then went into the kitchen to see if there was indeed a map. At first glance, I noticed nothing different. It looked as if I had been the last to have been in there. Nothing missing, nothing extra. The only thing that was large enough to hide anything was the Gold Cup 45. I quickly started taking the gun apart. I was sure it would be in the handle but I was wrong. Only someone that knew about a Colt 45 would know that the clip held seven bullets; Carson kept this gun with one in the chamber with the safety on. So far, the only space that I hadn't checked was the space at the bottom of the inside of the clip. I removed the six bullets left in the clip, and there it was, a tiny microchip inside a shell. At present, I have no way of checking the chip. Jack and I were done here. We closed up the house and returned to the airport via the same taxi.

Jack had flown the way over, I got to fly back. In all, we were on the ground for less than two hours. I would have liked to have flown over the sailing club, and flown high enough to see Sands and Elliot's key, but we again hugged the bay's smooth water then passed through the same Sand's Cut and out to the ocean. Once about 12 miles out I got a little more altitude. We had radio contact with Dan, and as we passed just to the north of Andros, got a visual of and spoke with Pearl and Johnny. Pearl and Johnny were flying Pearl's new T28. Pearl using her radio, asked how was the fishing? I said it was good. That I know of Pearl had no idea what we had been up to.

We had Pearl and Johnny's company only for a short time before asking for permission to land in Nassau. Pearl noted that she and Johnny were doing some spotting for Melody as Melody was assisting the locals in locating the conch migration. Conch was still one of Nassau attractions for the tourist. Our crawfish was still served on all the cruise ships, but to eat conch, one would have to put your feet on Bahamian ground. None of our boats brought in any conch; conch was still caught the old way by the small boats that used long poles with hooks or a net at the end. Just thinking about conch made me want to stop at Angee's on the way home. Ah, some good conch salad.

We wouldn't be taking any side trips on the way home; I was interested in getting home to get a good look at what we might have on the chip.

The girls were at what we all called home, Hill Top. Once there, Jack and I headed to the office. Our office was small, but we had just about everything but something that we could slip this chip into. I had thought about it and called our in-town boat repair shop. Carlos, our original Cuban that we had moved here some 18 years back to run the shop, said he would send over his machine that he used to look at engine semantics. Once the machine was here, we placed the chip in, and Wala, there it was. There was a handwritten note it read, "the CIA had planted Christina to locate the information that you and Carson were working on about the JFK assignation. When they sent Carson on a mission, they came and searched his house; they found nothing. They left and I came in. It took me less than an hour to find it; they were like a bull in a china cabinet. I looked for things that didn't belong. The concrete sealer, the drying powder, the extension bar, the large exhaust fan in the wall, the drain in the garage floor; how many two car garages had a drain in the bottom. I saw nothing in the house that gave any reason that Carson would keep that old car in running condition, even if it were a Mercedes".

I smiled as I read the note. I knew that Montibelli would have been there at least twice to have written this note and put it on a microchip.

I thought that whomever had helped Montibelli burry any treasure would still be there with the treasure; dead men don't talk. It was not the treasure that I thought of when I first saw Montibelli's will. Here on this note, there was an itemized list, there was lots and lots of jewelry, well over 1,200 items to include gems that hadn't as yet been made into jewelry, plenty of gold & silver, but the Crown Jewels were not on the list. All of the items listed had been placed in one of the Shah's Rolls Royce's. Montibelli's note told the story that while in exile, the Shah had stayed on Paradise Island. The Rolls and other items were being barged to Nassau, but as things happened, members of PLO had attacked the barge; the Ayatollah hired the PLO's Yasser Arafat to bring back the head of the Shah. Arafat had his men in Nassau waiting their chance while Arafat was looking for any wealth that could be gotten too. As it went, the attack on the barge resulted in the large limo falling overboard from the barge. The GPS coordinates, Montibelli wrote were not exact but should be close. Jack and I pulled the GPS coordinates on the computer, and bam, here we go again.

The excitement was more where the treasure was than the treasure itself. No more than 40 miles away lay a new adventure that a good portion of the family could participate in. Montibelli's closing note was in his native Arabic language. "Qad takun albadayie maeak," which meant, May the Gods be with you.

CHAPTER IV

THE TREASURE SEARCH

THE ATTACK OF THE SHAH'S barge had taken place just as it passed the northern end of Andros. The charts showed the water depth in that area at about 200 feet. Ten years later there might not be much of the car left; the currents could have easily covered up the car remains and the treasure goods. Jack noted that anything over 100 feet down, we would need a miniature submarine.

While Jack would locate and buy a two-person sub that could do the job, Dan and I would concentrate on finding the spot. Dan would use TESS to assist in the find while I would purchase a draggable camera system to film the bottom.

It was almost a month before we got in full gear, Dan and TESS had marked three good possible spots and one that was just to large to be ours. Since us starting might cause others to start looking in the same area, we chose to start with the largest spot. Here at the largest site we didn't need to drag the camera; we had TESS's exact GPS location. The barges were ready, but we would not move them until our find was clear. The small sub was placed on the north end of Andros, with Jack and I inside the sub; it was lifted and put down at the GPS coordinates that Dan gave us. Standing by near the same location was our 54 foot Ocean Sport, the "DEFIANCE". Aboard the "DEFIANCE" were Lori, Cindy, Carolina, Melody, and Sam. Dan, Pearl and Johnny were riding shotgun the air. Dan in the C-130 and Pearl and Johnny in Pearl's T28.

Jack and I were checked out on our small mini-sub. The toggle handle could move up to 100 pounds and lift 50. Our carry box would hold a maximum of 150 pounds of lift. The idea was to use the mini-sub's arm to attach a line to whatever we found so that the crew on the "DEFIANCE" could then hoist it up. Our hoist from our Panama trip had been reinstalled on the "DEFIANCE's" deck.

Certainly this was not Jacks first submarine trip, Jack had been a Navy Seal diver. Strangely enough it was not my first time either. Besides our short trainer. I too had been aboard a Navy Atomic powered sub. I was a Boy Scout, The USS NAUTILUS was visiting the Navy Base in Key West. We Scouts got a tour and our choice of ice cream.

Once the mini-sub was dropped in, the sub floated on its pontoons. We activated the dive, and the sub slowly descended.

Almost at once we saw what was at one time a good size yacht, Jack and I estimated 150 feet or more. This ship could have been down there for 50 or more years. It wasn't a navy vessel, more like some pleasure ship, maybe even one of the first passenger ships traveling to Nassau. All Jack and I could do was film what we saw. With all the fish life, it was hard to concentrate on the ship. Schools and schools of fish were swimming in, out and around the ship. A ship this size sinking would have to have someone looking for it. Even 50 years ago, I felt this ship should have been found. This ship hadn't just sunk; it looked to have been torpedoed!

We had been down there for less than an hour, it being only about 10:00 a.m., we would head to the following site. On our way to the next site we pass by a strange site. We were at about 190 feet or so; I had thought that conch only lived in shallow water; I was wrong about that! At our depth, we passed a large gathering of thousands. The next sight being only a mile away, we were there within the hour. This site was a small wreck of about 30 feet or so. It hadn't been down there long, but we could see that the cause of its sinking looked like it was from a fire. At a closer look, yes, the fire had sunk it, but it had been in a fight. We thought maybe it was one of the boats used by the PLO to attack the Shah's barge. Looking at the time and our next GPS spot, we surfaced, then told the girls that we would head to the next spot.

As we arrived we found a limo that was in fare shape, yes this was it. The rust hid most of the colors, but it was a black and tan Rolls. The Rolls had settled upside down sitting on its trunk. We gave it a push but it didn't budge. We photo'd the entire car then surfaced. I went aboard the "DEFIANCE" and used the computer. In minutes there appeared our two helicopters; one dropped a line to retrieve the mini-sub. The other would lift up Lori and myself. Yes Lori said she wanted to go with me so, I lifted her into the chair and hooked her up. The helicopter's crew hoisted her up, then sent the line back down for me. Jack would see to it that the "DEFIANCE" would get back to Nassau.

Lori and I had made it to the Government offices before they closed and made the three site claims and, yes, paid the $75,000 nonrefundable deposit, $25,000 for each find. Our new group of two young lawyers was there with us.

We would first move the two barges and using the mini-sub to hook up the Rolls. Once hooked the barges small hoist would be used to roll the Rolls onto it's tires. The tires seemed to be still holding air pressure. Using the barges in deeper waters would be more of a challenge; we had already thought of this and brought in four large anchors to hold the barges in place.

We wouldn't wait until Nassau sent their Coast Guard to mark the Rolls location. We hoped to be finished by the time they got around to marking it.

Almost a week passed, here we were again, ready to descend in the sub. The barges were in place, and the barge's electric hoist was ready with a cable and hook in the water. The barge's position wasn't perfect, but we thought it was good enough. We attempted to break a window but with no luck. The windows were bulletproof. We finally got the hook attached to a part of the car's right side bottom edge. We gave the operator on the barge the word and the car began to move. Funny how things don't always work out as you plan. The Rolls was lifted onto its side, but before it was sitting there on its own, the part that the hook was attached to broke off. This allowed the car to fall back down on its top. As the car fell, the door on the left rear had come some what open. This gave us another place to hook.

This time around the car was set up on its right side. As the car moved Jack and I could hear a shifting of the car's cargo. With weight shifting, the right rear fender crumbled just enough to permit us to get the hook into the trunk's lid. We hoped the car, when being further lifted, could fall to its tires, but what we got was the trunk's lid breaking off. With the car still sitting on its right side, when the trunk opened, several boxes appeared to fall out of the trunk. The hoist operator was told to back off. We unhooked the cable and told the hoist operator to raise the hook and send down a basket. As we waited for the basket, we used the sub's arm to remove more items from the trunk. By the time the basket was lowered, we had quite a pile of boxes.

We slowly started loading the boxes until our oxygen alarm sounded, warning us that our time was up. We had the hoist operator lift the basket. We backed away then surfaced. The sub was tethered and both Jack and I dove over and swam to the Ocean Sport.

The "DEFIANCE" had towed over the whaler; we used the whaler to get to the barges. There on the barge, sat the basket with the boxes that we had loaded from the bottom. My hart hadn't beat so hard in quite some time. Lori, still aboard the "DEFIANCE," yelled out, well, what are you waiting for? One of the barge crew brought out a small tool that resembled a crowbar. I lifted out the first box and saw that I would need a small chisel and hammer. I placed the first box on the steel deck then began to open the box. With Jack's help, we managed to open the well-built, still intact box.

When opening the box, there nicely sealed in plastic was our first treasure find. It was a gold neckless filled with sparkling jewels. This neckless wasn't like any neckless we had found from our Drake's treasure. This looked, well, too beautiful for anyone to put on. I took the neckless and held it up so that Lori could get a look. Lori's reaction was to ask, yelling if it was real? I yelled back, yes.

I wouldn't waste time opening another box; I was now interested in getting the sub ready to return to the bottom.

In all, today, Jack and I had made two more trips down to the car's trunk. We now had 46 boxes on board the Barges. The sub was set up for night driving, but I felt it unsafe. The weather had now changed some what and we began to have small swells. We called in the helicopters, one would lift out the sub and place it on the barge's deck. Once the sub was aboard the barge and secured, the treasure was lifted aboard the two copters. This time Jack and Cindy went back with the copters and the treasure.

With some concern about the weather, I used the computer and requested a TESS up date. Dan was up there with the C-130 and said the wind had picked up but nothing that the "DEFIANCE" and the barges couldn't weather. I decided to pull up anchor on the "DEFIANCE" and, with the whaler in tow, head-on into Nicholls Town. We would pass through the northeast channel and anchor for the night on the shore side of the reef.

Going through the northeast channel had me remembering my first trip here with Rusty in the "PRINCESS." Back then, when Rusty and I crossed the reef, we didn't need to use the channel. At that time, the "PRINCESS" glided over the reef as Rusty watched that beautiful bottom through our seat's glass-bottom window. Rusty and I had anchored then swam over the reef, reaching that straight down drop off at the reef's edge. At the time, it was the most beautiful sight I'd ever seen. Straight down the reef's edge, there were fish everywhere! I remember that had I swam out past the edge of the reef looking down and could see a giant shark swimming down there amongst all the other fish. I knew that the shark could come up and eat me, but why would it when it had so much food swimming around it. Rusty, on the other hand, was in his panic mode. In the water he was waving me to come back. I obliged, turning around to make the return swim—what a memory.

Lori and I would anchor closer to the reef than shore. We, too, would swim over the reef to the edge. I didn't carry a speargun, but a 12 gage bang stick. Lori of course was a swimmer, a champion swimmer I was reminded. The reef's drop off was the same, it was a beautiful sight to see. Lori looked like she wanted to stay but I reminded her it was a shark's feeding time. I could see her eye brow raise as we turned back.

This side of Andros blocked most of the wind that had picked up, but soon after we returned to the "DEFIANCE," the water's rolls started getting worse. Lori and I decided to use the whaler and headed south along the shore; we would stop at Lucy's hotel thinking of getting a room. We would still need to anchor the whaler a short distance from shore and swim in.

Lucy was happy to see us both and found dry clothes for us. My old room was available, as were most of the others. Since the moving of both vehicles to Homestead, business had slowed down quite a bit. Lori and I hadn't been back since we had sold our Dock House property to the Navy and donated both dig sights to the Bahamian Government. Both dig sights were being readied to become national parks. The northern sight, the possible first landing sight of Columbus. The southern sight is an incredible burial sight of the Seminole Indians that had migrated from South Florida. The Seminoles had come from south Florida in canoes looking for refuge from the war. The Seminoles were the only Indian group not to have surrendered to the American Soldiers.

Lori and I got that good shower, I remembered the first several showers I had here were with saltwater. That was until our group remodeled the place.

Dinner was much the same as years back; we were served a whole baked fish. Lori mentioned that it had been years since she picked through the fish bones. Lori was reminiscing of her past days of cleaning the fishermen's boats and mostly being paid in fish. Lori quietly mentioned that we should have brought with us a few crawfish.

Lucy said that still, the fishermen talked about Lusca, and some still believed it was still out there. Of course, Lucy inquired what had brought us here, Lori not mentioning the treasure, said that we had found an old wreck just a few miles off the northern coast. We hadn't heard much from Lucy's father until then. Lucy's father said that he remembered when he heard a story that a ship had gone down in those waters. Lucy's father said that at least one lifeboat was said to have made it to shore. It was Lusca, they said, a great sea monster that had sunk the ship. Lucy's father said the lifeboat was still down at the fishing village; the fishermen, he said, had turned it into a fishing boat. No motor, of course; it's a rowing boat. I'm sure I can find the boat tomorrow if you'd like to see it, he said. Yes, I said we can ride down there tomorrow in the whaler.

The following day after breakfast, the 4 of us swam out to the whaler, pulled up anchor, and headed north. We motored on by the "DEFIANCE" that was at anchor and continued heading north. When arriving at the fishing village, we anchored and swam into shore. Lucy's father was well known at the fishing village. He spoke to a few men, and we were pointed to the boat we were looking for. The boat, about 14 feet long had 4 sets of oar locks, the oar locks looked to be originals. On the stern, I could barely make out the word "FORTUNA"; it was the Spanish name for Fortune.

As we surveyed the boat, an old man strolled up, offering a story. It was late in the year 1953 he said, we were out fishing when I spotted the boat, we thought they were all dead, he said. There were nine body's aboard. As we moved the boat, blood and seawater rushed from one side to the other, almost turning it over. Then we saw her move; it was a child. She seemed unharmed but looked to be in shock. We took her aboard and then checked the others. The others were dead; it looked like they all had been shot, yes the old man said, they had all been shot, not just once, several times.

We took the boat in tow back to the village. We cared for the girl and buried the others. The girl, I asked, what became of her? Did she say what had happed to the others? The old man then said that the girl never spoke a word. She was odd-looking with a larger-looking head and deformed feet. We took her to the Navy base he said. That's the end of the story, he said; you're the first person to come to look at the boat or interested to hear my story. What about the dead peoples belongings I asked? Truthfully the old man said we sold what jewelry the women had and the men's watches all but one. There was money too, the old man said, not much but enough to build me and my two brothers' houses. What about identification or paperwork, I asked? Sorry the older man said, I only have the one watch. I only kept the watch because it had the words, Submariner, on it, and it said it was waterproof. Do you still have the watch I asked? The old man looked at me and asked, you're not going to take it from me, are you? No Sir, I said, the watch is yours, I just want to see if it has an inscription on the back. Yes the older man said, but I could not understand what it said. Wait here the old man said and I will bring the watch. While the old man walked away, I looked at the boat. I took out my knife and dug into one of the holes that I thought just might have been a bullet hole. What I dug out was what I was sure was a 45 caliber slug. There were other holes; the few I dug out were all from the same caliber weapon.

The old man returned with the watch, sure enough it was a Submariner Rolex. The inscription on the back looked to be in Latin. What I was sure of was the name on the bottom of the inscription, Maximus! Lori took the watch; she had heard the older man's description of the girl and had my exact thought. Lori said she thought it said "Commander, my right hand, thanks, Maximus". Lori handed the watch back to the old man; Lori then asked, would you sell it to me? Oh no mam the old man said. Then he quickly asked how much she would pay? Lori said she would give him a new watch, the same mark but new plus 1,000 dollars. The old man said $2,000 and the same watch. Lori said it was a deal. The old man smiled. I then said that I would like to buy the boat. The old man smiled and said that he didn't go out fishing anymore. Then asked another $2,000. It's a deal, I said and held out my hand. Lori said she'd have the money and watch here by tomorrow afternoon. It was strange I thought, I had been to this same village some years back, I didn't mention it in present company, this because the time that I was here was just after Lucy and Carla had been attacked by the Navy personnel. Back then, I had also purchased a boat's stern and, of course, the tooth that was said to have been left stuck in what was left of it's stern. Yes, Lusca had attacked the small boat and killed all aboard.

This time as we passed the "DEFIANCE," we dropped off Lori so she could start the process for the exchange of money, the watch, and the boat.

The seas were still rougher than normal so Lori would also cancel today's dive. Dan, of course, would keep vigilance over the area to include the "DEFIANCE."

Once I returned to the "DEFIANCE", Lori and I were able to talk. I used the computer to contact Jerry; this was a perfect case for him and his people. I knew we were still on Mr. Rodgers, but I didn't know if we had a contact number for him. Jerry said that Mr. Rodgers was in a hotel in Canada. Jerry said that contacting Mr. Rodgers would blow whatever surveillance we had going on. I said that I needed him back in Nassau. Jerry said he understood and would make contact. My next communication would be with Jack, Jack said the treasure drop-off at the bank went well. The Treasure still in wooden boxes had all but filled the bank's vault.

Jack said it would take another 24 hours for the seas to clam and another 24 to settle the bottom.

We pulled up anchor and would head on back to Nassau. We would reach the Nassau docks by mid-afternoon. During our trip to Nassau, Lori and I had plenty of time to plan the next steps. First was to find what had happened to the girl turned over to the Navy. We didn't want to cause too much attention, but we had to find her. We needed to find more about the ill-fated ship. At least a manifest with a passenger list. Maybe we could find a young girl on the list.

Next, we would contact a barge with a crane from Miami. The crane would need to lift the Shah's entire car to the barge. It was understood that Jack and I would need to dive with the mini-sub at least another day before the barge arrived and then again the day the crane arrived to hook up the car to the crane's hook.

By night fall, via phone I had reached Mr. Rodgers, inviting him back to Nassau. I told him that I had news that would interest him. He, of course, was hesitant but agreed to come.

From Miami, I contacted my old friend Bob. Due to Bob's cancer fight, his teaching days at the UM were finished. Of course, he still had his export company and the managing percent of the shipping company. I felt terrible that we hadn't seen Bob in so long. I told Bob that we had stumbled onto a sunken ship named FORTUNA. I asked that he research any information that he or his UM friends could find. Who knows, maybe we will find that it was carrying something special. Bob sounding weak said he would be happy to help. Bob then mentioned that he wanted a sit down with me to discuss selling me his business shares. I told him whenever he was ready just to let me know.

Two days later, we all returned to the barges. The mini-sub was lifted back into the water. Jack and I spent the day cleaning out the Rolls's trunk, this time moving gold and silver bars. The weather was holding and by 6:00 p.m. Jack and I had done all we could.

The pile of boxes, gold and silver bars piled on the barge's deck was a sight to see. The helicopters would now have to make at least two trips moving the treasure to Nassau. The boxes hadn't made anyone question what we had, but these bars would be seen on the dock, and the word of another treasure would spread like wildfire.

Lori had made arrangements with the bank; tonight, they would stay open until our last load was in. It was 11:00 p.m. before we finished. Jack was ashore in Nassau, Lori and I stayed aboard the "DEFIANCE."

We had received notice that the barge with the crane should be at sight by daybreak. We were cutting it close. Thus far, we hadn't had much ship traffic, but given the news of an immense treasure find, even the cruise ships would now change their timing and route to pass close enough so that the passengers could see what a treasure site looked like. There wasn't much to see, but just the thought of a treasure find was enough. Then there were the people that would know what we had found. The Iranians would undoubtedly want their treasures back. Bahamian law was crystal clear. Finder's keepers, of course, the Bahamians would get their 25%.

The barge arrived, and with one dive with the mini-sub, Jack and I had the Rolls hooked up and on its way up from the ocean's bottom. Jack and I made sure that nothing had been left on the bottom or that anything fell from the car. The car was placed on one of our two barges. The barge with the crane would head on back to Miami while our Nassau tug boat would now tow our two barges back to Nassau. Our operation was done out here. One of the copters had picked up the mini-sub, and the four of the crew and us in the "DEFIANCE" would ride alongside the tug towing our barges.

Once arriving in Nassau, the Rolls would be lifted off the barge and loaded onto the pier. We could now inspect what was left of and in the car. We were pleasantly pleased to find another 500 pounds of gold placed under the back seat floorboards.

In all, the Bahamian Government settled with Lori on their 25%, that amount being $30,000,000. When I heard the amount, I thought but didn't say that we should have let Bob make the money deal with the Government. I didn't know at the time that Lori had sent the Shah's oldest son a photo of the jeweled neckless. The Shah's oldest son had offered $150,000,000 for the over one thousand pounds of jewels and Jewelry. At market value, Lori said we had over $72,000,000 in gold and silver. Again I was surprised Lori didn't take the Shah's son's offer.

At home I had left a message that I wanted to have a sit down with Pearl, the sit down was threefold. First of all, the pilots of the C-130 that were assigned to watch out for her reported that Pearl had twice in one week flown into Cuban air space. The pilots said that they were not close enough to have given any assistance should Cuba have sent out any of their MiGs. Pearl said that the Cuban's didn't even pick her up on their radar. Pearl did, however, promise that she would keep her skinny tail out of harm's way. Pearl said at least until she could "defend herself."

That brought us to the second thing. I had been informed that she was shopping for a Harrier Jet. Pearl said that she felt that she had graduated into a jet and that the Harrier was something that could take off and land on any hard surface with a clear radius of 100 feet. Pearl agreed that she wouldn't buy such a jet without my approval. The third item was about what we had discovered about the sunken ship and its only survivor. With this news, Pearl changed her focus and agreed that we must find the little girl.

I cautioned that if that little girl had been eight years old then, she could now be about 45. I added that it would have been hard to have hidden her secret all these years. I let her know that this didn't change anything of our agreement to speak with no one, not anyone, about who her birth parents were.

Pearl was informed that Mr. Rodgers was on his way to Nassau, me telling her that as far as we knew, Mr. Rodgers was the last one to see and speak with Maximus. Pearl then admitted that she was sure that TESS would have informed us if Maximus wasn't still alive. I told Pearl that Rodgers had been checked out and I intended to bring him into our group.

Lori had made good on our promise to the old fisherman, and I then showed Pearl the watch that the old fisherman said he had taken from one of the bodies from the sunken ship's lifeboat. Pearl looked at the watch and then said, "the Commander, he knew Maximus." Yes I said, I believed that it was not a coincidence that the Commander and the little girl were searched out. I was sure that the ship had been sunk by the same people that had killed the Commander and the group in the lifeboat. For all we know, the little girl's entire family could have been on that lifeboat, including the Commander.

Pearl was to stay in the background while Rodgers was here in Nassau. I asked her not to make a show. Bob too would be here. Bob was bringing with him the sunken ship's manifest. Our workshop meeting would be at Bob's old beach house.

Jerry had been sent the manifest and already had quite a bit of news for us.

CHAPTER V

THE "FORTUNA"

SECURITY WAS HIGH, IN ATTENDANCE were Lori, Jerry, Rodgers, Bob, Jack, and myself. Jerry had found the ship's information, the "FORTUNA" was owned by a military contractor named "Bellator Corporation". Bellator was a fast-moving developer of a laser system that was said could have revolutionized modern warfare. The corporation was started in 1948 and by 1953 was testing such a laser system with the US Army. Jerry said the testing was abruptly canceled when the owner and top designer disappeared while aboard the "FORTUNA." Jerry said that the " FORTUNA" had been anchored in the Havana harbor for three days before departing for the Bahamas. The "FORTUNA" was never seen or heard from again. The company was the sole owner of one man, Mr. John Smith. Mr. & Mrs. Smith we're aboard the "FORTUNA" with their 7-year old daughter at the time of their disappearance. There were nine crew members and 24 passengers aboard when the "FORTUNA" left Havana. The ship nor any survivors have ever been found, Jerry said. Until now, I said. We have located the ship at the bottom of the ocean. There were at least eight survivors that had gotten on and launched a lifeboat. The lifeboat was tracked down an the occupants were executed with I believe was a Thomson 45 calibrator machine gun.

I told the group that in 1953 Eisenhower had just become President; before being elected, Eisenhower, while campaigning, warned that defense contractors were becoming too powerful. Hover heard the to be President's words. Bellator only being a company for 5 years was then worth more than the next five defense company's put together. Bellator's start-up money had not gone unnoticed; Hover thought the money could have been coming from some of our adversaries.

In a flash, all was lost. The company Bellator had no heirs and was liquidated in favor of the U.S. Government. Jerry said that we must agree that with the disappearance of Mr. Smith, the laser development seemed to have disappeared with him.

Rodgers looked at me and asked where we had gotten that information? We all laughed. I looked at Rodgers and asked if he was interested in joining our small group? Rodgers said that even though our Government had stolen everything that he had, he was still a patriot. I said that we all loved our country. However, its people are not always given the truth. It's the Government that we don't trust to make the right decisions. It's the corrupt few that we worry about; we, I said, are all patriots.

How does all of this connect with myself and Maximus, Rodgers asked? I then handed Rodgers the watch. Rogers took the watch and asked, you think Mr. Smith knew Maximus? I believe they were brothers; I answered—Brothers from an extraordinary family. Rodgers looked at us and asked, TESS? I have heard that the Government has been testing something called TESS Rodgers said. Is this from the same family? Yes I said. Is Maximus the last of the family? No I said, Mr. Smith, the Commander, had a daughter that survived the "FORTUNA." She'd be about 45 years old and could be institutionalized, or Maximus could have somehow gotten her. I asked Rodgers if he had ever seen Maximus with or if he had ever mentioned a niece or daughter? No, Rodgers said; it was only Maximus. No wife, no daughter, no family.

I looked at Rodgers and asked how close he was to having a flying machine ready. Rodger told us what we already knew. He was working in a small warehouse in Canada. Rodgers said he felt that money was his only holdback, and he was sure that Uncle Sam was watching him. By what you've told me, Rodger's said, once I have the craft ready, they'd just come for it. Yes, I said, and you. Are you offering something here, Rodgers asked? Yes, we would like to move your shop to Paxi and become partners with your craft. I believe we have the two items you lack, the money and a computer system with a built-in guidance system. We also have the laser system that the Commander was working on. I added that for the last several months, we had a security team watching over him. Security will be tight; you can come and go as you wish, the information and design you now have are yours, and you could, at a future date, go on your own or join another group. However, I said, any information you gain from this point on will be tightly held and not shared. Rodgers said he understood and agreed.

Rodgers said he would join our group. From our meeting, Jack would accompany Rodgers to Paxi then back to Canada.

Our next step was to find the Commander's daughter.

It was almost two months before Rodgers and his shop was set up in Paxi. Of course Pearl had made her introduction. Pearl went nowhere without her pilot's headgear on. At first, she wore the headgear to help hide her big bald head. Nowadays, Pearl doesn't take it off.

Pearl had heard Mr. Rodgers's story of the light weight material that Maximus had put together. Pearl said that she would ask TESS to help her out. TESS only gave her a riddle to solve. Pearl said that she wasn't in the mood for games.TESS only repeated the riddle.

It wasn't long before Pearl and Rodgers were working side by side. Soon they had changed several of the body parts of the already modified T28. The change produced an increase of speed by almost 30%.

It didn't take long before Pearl asked about the Harrier.

We were three months out before we hit pay dirt looking for the Commander's daughter. Although we believed we had found her, she was locked behind closed doors. Turned out many wealthy families that had troubled or handicapped children. In this case, the US Government had the Commander's daughter committed to a mental institute for the criminally insane. We didn't know if they knew whom they had or just locked her up because she was unresponsive and odd. Either way, we made a plan and hoped for the best. We got ourselves a group of lawyers representing her, claiming that the Government had deprived her of her rights. The Case was booked as Jane Doe Vs. the U.S. Government. The institute that housed her claimed that their Jane Doe could not speak and did not know right from wrong. For our side to have a better chance of proving otherwise, we appealed to TESS to get our message to Maximus. The response was almost immediate; Maximus would meet Pearl, Lori, and me.

The next day while the three of us waited on the porch of our Harbor Island House, a craft hovered then landed on the beach. The craft was small and had the shape more like an upside-down "V" than a circle. A side hatch opened, and out stepped a man wearing an odd suit and helmet; we started walking his way, then Pearl began to run at him. By the time Pearl got to the man, he had taken off his helmet and opened his arms to receive Pearl. When Lori and I got to them, Pearl introduced the man as her uncle Maximus. Maximus, without removing his gloves, shook our hands as I introduced Lori and myself.

We had anticipated the visit and had set up a beach tarp and chairs. I mentioned that TESS was up there watching and that this side of the Island had been secured. Maximus said that it was not possible that TESS nor any other radar had picked him up traveling inbound. Maximus said his small ship was designed using a technology called stealth. The stealth design and material use, he said, made it impossible to be seen by radar.

I didn't pay much attention to what he said as the meeting was not about his advances but the plan to get the Commander's daughter freed. I explained my plan, and Maximus agreed. Maximus said his niece's name was Majstro in Latin, Star in English. My brother and his wife called her Sunshine, he said.

We all agreed that Hover didn't discover who the Commander really was. If they had, they would have taken him alive. They only saw him as a threat.

Maximus was well known; he had worked for NASA and IBM; if he showed up in all of this, I believed that they, being our Government, would have a better chance of putting all the pieces together. I was a known treasure hunter and, while searching for the Shah's treasure, had stumbled onto the "FORTUNA." No, we couldn't risk Maximus nor Pearl showing up in any of this. I was looking for something that the Commander's daughter could recognize. Maximus said that it would be the song "you are my Sunshine, my only Sunshine" Maximus said that Star's parents sang that song to her almost every day. Maximus was sure that if anything would catch Star's attention, it would be that song.

At the end of the short meeting, Maximus said that he would like to barrow Pearl for a few days, I would have ok'd the trip, but

Pearl said no. Then out of the blue Pearl went on the attack. Uncle she asked, why didn't you search for your brother when he and his family went missing? Surely you could have found them. Then Pearl asked why he hadn't searched out his sister or offered more assistance when she came looking for her husband? Maximus then said that he had hired a plane and searched for the missing ship everyday for week. Leaving Havana and having the ship's route, there was only one answer, the ship and all aboard had been lost. Your mother showed up at my office, I hadn't seen her in over 20 years. She was looking for her husband and didn't even ask about our brother. I told her what I knew and she left, just like that. I knew nothing about my sister having a baby daughter. I didn't know if your mother found her husband or not; I never heard from her again. I then asked, do you have the vehicle? Did Victoria leave your father's ship with you? Maximus said he knew nothing about his father's ship except it was lost at the bottom of the TOTO channel in 1946. If so, I asked how did you communicate with TESS? TESS found me he said. The only thing I knew about TESS was that it used our family's signature. TESS arranged this meeting, then Maximus asked that if we didn't have the a ship where did we get the Computer system from? I then made a long story as short as I could.

Then Maximus asked what we would do with Star once we got her back? Pearl stepped in saying that we will take her as family. Maximus then said that if his father's ship wasn't equipped with its original computer, then it couldn't be trusted to follow Victoria's orders. We must find the ship and restore the original computer, Maximus said. Pearl then said that she trusted Victoria's judgment and would wait until the Vehicle came for her.

Maximus, still zipped up in his entire bodysuit, began to look like he struggled to breathe. Maximus kissed Pearl on the head and said he would keep in touch. Maximus turned and started walking to his small ship; he then turned, looking at Lori, and commented that my taste in women was exceptional. He then turned and entered his ship; after the hatch closed, the ship took off almost straight up into the sun's light and disappeared.

Pearl then looked at me and asked what I thought? About the Song I said, I hope it works. And about my uncle Pearl asked, do you believe him? I smiled and said that in a short time we will know where his heart is. Pearl then looked at Lori and said that her uncle was right about one thing. The Captain she said, I mean the Colonel has exception taste in women. The three of us then hugged.

Maximus was right about another thing, none of our radar had picked up Maximus as he flew in or out. TESS only picked up Maximus when he had taken off his helmet. I said the suit and helmet must have also had some of the Stealth design to them. Pearl said that after we got Sunshine out from where she was and safely home, she would get her hands on some of the stealth stuff.

CHAPTER VI

SUNSHINE

FOUR DAYS LATER, THE LAWYERS, I, and a translator that spoke Latin found ourselves sitting in front of a judge and this very odd-looking middle-aged woman. The woman whom we would now call Sunshine had been brought in with her hands cuffed. I immediately stood and demanded the cuffs be removed; the judge signaled me to be seated and ordered the cuffs removed.

The judge then read from a script that explained that this was a preliminary hearing to see if Jane Doe was as unresponsive as the Institute where she had been placed said she was. The judge looked at the woman and asked if she had understood what she had said? The women just looked forward. May we talk to her judge, I asked? The judge said to go ahead. Our translator then spoke in Latin, saying that we were friends of her parents, hear to take her home. At first, the woman didn't even look our way. The Translator then said that we were told by her uncle Maximus that her name was Sunshine and that her parents would sing her this song. I looked at her and started signing the "you are my Sunshine" song. All at once, the woman said in plain English, yes, I'm Sunshine. The translator quickly said in Latin not to repeat anything here that had happened to herself and her family. The judge then asked not to speak anymore in the translator's language. The judge then looked at Sunshine and asked, what is your full name? Sunshine looked at the judge and said, my name is Star Smith, I was on a boat with my family when it sank, and my family and I were separated. Sunshine continued saying that she had been locked up for many years and now she wanted to leave with these people. The judge looked to be in shock. The judge said that Sunshine was to be placed in the care of her attorneys until a hearing could be set to have Sunshine permanently freed. Sunshine stood even before the judge could finish, Sunshine was coming to me. I looked at her and said she was going home; Sunshine had tears rolling down her face as she hugged me, saying she had waited so long for someone to come. Myself, now standing, looked at the judge and asked, may we go now? The judge said we would have a few papers to sign, but Sunshine would not wait another hour before being a free woman.

It was that same day and without any permission from the court that Sunshine was boarded on our Leer and flown straight to Nassau. You probably figured that I had come into the country under the radar. I'd been flown into Tamiami airport, then I took a train to Jacksonville, then a taxi to the facility where Sunshine had been held. Exiting from Jacksonville, I accompanied Sunshine on the Leer.

The once little girl did not look or express fear; she held my hand and did not let go the entire trip.

At the Nassau airport, we had arranged Sunshine's entrance to avoid going through customs. It was the first in some time that I had seen Pearl in public not wearing her pilot's headgear. I was sure it was to have Sunshine see and notice that she was with one of her own. Sunshine didn't look as good as she felt; over the years, her spine had taken a slight curve that added to her age. Sunshine was now 46 years old, spending almost 37 years in that one lockdown facility. When Sunshine laid her eyes on Pearl, Sunshine let a loud sigh that the entire airport could hear. Sunshine's sigh then turned into tears. Pearl, now having both arms around Sunshine, both started with tears; of course, Lori was right there crying right with them. Pearl and Sunshine spoke in Latin, but then Sunshine stopped and looked at Lori in good English and said, Hello, friend. Then the three girls hugged each other, holding hands as we walked to the cars. Once in the car, Sunshine's attention turned to Pearl's gold bracelet; in Latin, Sunshine asked Pearl if that bracelet was hers? Sunshine said that she was wearing that same bracelet on the day they had been attacked. Pearl then took the bracelet off and placed it on Sunshine's left wrist. For the first time, Sunshine's deep blue eyes sparkled. Lori and I both knew that the bracelet was Pearl's as both Victoria and Pearl had been wearing matching bracelets that day we met them both. When we received Pearl, she was wearing this same bracelet. Pearl had just given away her only item linking her to her mother, Victoria.

Once at Hill Top, June and Betty were at the door to welcome us. It was the strangest thing; Sunshine hugged June like they were old friends. The children were there and had taken Sunshine's hand, wanting to show her around the house. Of course, Sunshine would be bunking with Pearl.

It would be days before Sunshine relived the time that her father's ship was attacked. Sunshine said there had been a loud explosion, and it seemed that the ship went down very fast. Her father had gotten one of the small boats that had been on deck into the water just as the ship's bowl pointed upward then disappeared into the ocean. Sunshine said that it didn't seem real; the seas were calm.

All of a sudden, everyone else was gone. Sunshine then said a boat appeared, and her father was standing waving his shirt. The boat came our way, and once upon us, a man stood with a large gun and shot my father several times, then turning the gun on my mother and the others. My mother had turned her back and threw me to the bottom of the boat falling on me. The next thing I remembered was the fishermen pulling me from the others; my father and mother were among the dead. Sunshine said she would never forget the man's face that held the gun, never she repeated.

I thought that if they had been sent by Hover, it could be easy to get photos of the men that, in those days could have done the dirty work. Jerry had already been working on this.

Our now President was now about 66 years old, 37 years ago he would have been only 29. Sunshine said the the men on the boat that killed her parents were in their upper 30s to mid-forties. No, I thought this deed didn't have his mark, as was the case ten years later.

Pearl said she wanted in on locating those responsible for her uncle's death and locking Sunshine away. I reminded Pearl that those in power then would no longer be alive. Hover had died some 18 years back. Since then, six presidents had come and gone. Pearl said that the man that pulled the trigger could still be alive, and she would find him and bring him and others to justice. If he's out there we will find him I said. One day we will also find the last one of Lucy's attackers and the two others that Murdered Montibelli. One day I said, one day soon.

CHAPTER VII

KUWAIT

A T THE END OF JULY, those same two Mossad friends of Bob showed up in Nassau. They weren't trying to buy TESS; they asked for our assistance. The Israelis said that Husain of Iraq was about to invade Kuwait. They wanted our C130s to ride shot gun over the Iraq, Kuwait border. The Israelis said that Kuwait would pay for the protection. I thought and asked, why would Husain believe that the U.S. and others would allow his intrusion into Kuwait? The two Israelis said that the U.S. ambassador had just met with her Iraq counterpart, assuring the Iraqis that the U.S. Government did not want conflict with Iraq and had no treaty to defend Kuwait. This the Israelis said was the go-ahead for Husain. The invasion will happen within days they said. I told the Israelis that to decide to do such a thing would take days, if not weeks, only to think about. I told them that it would be impossible to gear up with what we would need to protect Kuwait in less than a month. The Israelis then said that then Husain would not be stopped and would within the week have his hold on Kuwait.

I didn't feel the need to explain to the Israelis my views; I thought that us stopping the Iraqis without us losing men and equipment was improbable. Besides if the Iraqis were stopped, them loosing most

55

if not all of their air power and a significant number of their tanks. Then their foes, the Iranians, might muster up an attack on Iraq, starting their war again. The outcome of a second Iran Iraq war might then allow Iran's revolution to spread. Kuwait may be saved from one evil only to be swallowed up by another. No, we would stay home from this one. Besides, somehow, I thought I would or could have a lot to lose at home.

On August the second, Husain invaded Kuwait; it only took the Iraqis two days to control Kuwait. All of the monarchy and what was left of the Kuwait armed forces exited into Saudi Arabia. No other countries lifted a hand to stop Husain from annexing Kuwait as a new part of Iraq. While this was happening, I did some checking; Husain claimed that while he fought the war to stop Iran's revolutionary spread to Iraq and its neighbors, the Kuwait monarch loaned vast amounts of money to Iraq to continue the war. Husain had been claiming for months that while he was waging war, Kuwait had been stealing his oil. Yes, Husain said that he could show the world that Kuwait had dug oil wells that started on Kuwait's side of the border but were dug at a slant to reach into Iraq's oil base. Yes, Kuwait had drilled what was called slant wells, and yes, it appeared that Husain may have been right. Husain had wanted Kuwait to forgive the billions of Iraq's debt, plus Husain wanted Kuwait to stop the theft. The Mossad pair hadn't explained all of this, even though they surely knew. Of course, I had told Jack and Dan that the Israelis were asking, and of course, we also looked how fast we could gear up for something like this if we had chosen to.

Of course the Iraq invasion happen even before we had gathered even 20% of the information we needed. We had two first generation model TESS units that had been removed from the C-130s that were now being used in Jerry's commercial air business, plus the two C-130s with TESS that we still operated. Such a mission would need

Jerry's units refitted with the first generation TESS, plus we would need the newest TESS models and two or three more C-130s. If even possible, it would take months for G.D. to produce the equipment we would need. Plus, at a glance, the only C-130s that were on the market were older stuff with high engine hours. The price of a new C-130 was about $23,000,000, and the first one couldn't be delivered for six months out. Then there would be outfitting it with what it would take to support TESS. We have a high stake in G.D., controlling several of their production products. If you counted Jena's stock and the newly acquired Montibelli stock, our group, according to Lori, were among the largest G.D. stockholders. Lockheed Martin was another story; there, we couldn't place an order without the Military and the President knowing. We were presently well stocked with C-130 parts for our two planes plus if we needed more, there was a large black market of such parts.

Lori didn't know about the Mossad visit but did find out about some of our inquiries. She expressed her concerns, which made things between us somewhat complex, even though we hadn't ordered anything.

CHAPTER VIII

BOB'S DEATH

BOB NEVER GOT TO MEET Sunshine, not even Pearl; Bob died in his sleep only two months later. Bob had the same wife ever since I had known him; he had two daughters that I had never met, nor had Bob 'ever talked about them. Bob's Miami funeral was the largest I had ever been to. I shouldn't have gone, but nothing could have kept me away. I wasn't invited to the funeral nor asked to talk at Bob's funeral, but still, when I got the chance, I walked to the pulpit and talked. I said that Bob had been a friend of mine since I was fifteen. I said I loved him ever since. I then paused and laughed and said that I started living when I met Bob. Bob, I said, was full of life and adventures. Bob was a true friend that would do anything for his country or a friend. When I closed my eyes last night, I said, I saw and heard Bob; he had that same Cuban Cigar in his hand and that laugh that just made you smile. Bob once spent a month in a Cuban jail, Bob said that if Castro had cut his supply of Cuban Cigars off, he might have buckled and given them what they wanted. I then was the only one to laugh. Bob I said, I love you and will truly miss you. I then stepped from the pulpit and walked straight to the outside door.

From the church door to my waiting car, from the vehicle to the Tamiami airport, and into the guarded T28 that Pearl had lent me for the trip. I had no copilot; it was just me. I was supposed to fly down low, the way I had come in, only causing a ripple in the water as I passed by. I took off and as my landing gear came up, I pushed the throttle forward. The plane seemed to glide through the air. Instead of staying low, I went high enough to see the Sand's Key cove and the artificial cut and lake into the island's interior. Then I came back around and flew along the western side of Elliot's Key and south to Billy's point. From Billy's point, I swooped down and turned east and flew just at the treetops going through Caesar's creek. In the blink of an eye, I was flying east just 15 or 20 feet above the sea. My speed was now just over 400 MPH. Dan was up there covering me with one of the C-130s; I heard his voice saying they could not locate me on their radar. I laughed and thought that now I knew how Pearl felt when she was flying this thing.

June was at the Nassau airport when I arrived; both she and Lori had discovered that I had gone without permission. June had been at the airport waiting since she heard the news. June was dress in a black dress, and for the first time in some time, I looked at her and once again saw a more than a beautiful woman.

CHAPTER IX

SUNSHINE'S RECOVERY

WE HAD A SPECIALIST FROM the U.K. flown in to work with Sunshine on her spine curvature. The specialist said that wearing the brace that she provided, Sunshine would make a full recovery. The brace reminded me of the brace that my first friend had worn when he and his family had returned from Cuba. My friend Carlos's uncle was the ex-president of Cuba. When Castro overthrew Batista, Prio believed that Castro would abide by their private agreement. You see, Prio had quietly provided the arms and financial support for Castro's revolution. When Castro came into power, Prio took his entire family back to Cuba, including my friend Carlos. Four long years later my friend returned to Miami as a refugee. Carlos hadn't been confined as Sunshine was, but the mistreatment and food they were given contributed to his ill health. Carlos wore his brace for more than a year and did recover. Sunshine didn't like the brace but didn't complain, at least not to me.

Time flew by and Thanksgiving was at our door. We all had lots to give thanks for. Sunshine was doing well making the adjustments, even helping around the house.

The Shah's treasure was appraised at over $350,000,000. Lori had sold just one neckless for $27,000,000. The buyer didn't say to whom the neckless was for but I believed it was bound for the Shah's wife. The price of Gold was at an all time high and Lori wanted to store some and sell the rest. I asked if she was going to bury what she wasn't going to sell?

Pearl spent a lot of time in Paix working with Rodgers. The two of them seemed to be working well together. Pearl said they, her, and Rodgers wanted my approval to buy that Harrier that she had mentioned. The purchase was approved but without armament. I had that personal experience with what Pearl had done with her T28; she had made it lighter, faster, and almost impossible to be picked up on radar.

We hadn't, that I knew of, had any contact from Pearl's uncle Maximus. Surly, Maximus had heard that we had recovered Sunshine. I was sure he would have shown up to visit with her but he had not. We hadn't talked about it but I thought Maximus didn't look well. Maybe he just needed some sun. Pearl had, of course, talked about their uncle to Sunshine. Sunshine wanted to meet and speak with her uncle. However, Sunshine seemed content with what she had.

CHAPTER X

THE SAUDI'S VISIT

Two weeks before Christmas Lori said she and the children would spend Christmas in General Santos. Our son Gary was now 3 and Joe-Anne 1. I hoped that Lori was figuring that I, too, would want to go along not to miss the children's Christmas. I wouldn't say I liked how Lori took it on her own to plan the trip. I didn't want her to go, but I would not stop her. Without telling Melody nor Sam that I was not going along, they, along with Chubby and Lilly, had signed on for the trip. Melody and Sam came to me together saying that if I didn't go, they weren't going. Sam said that if Gary could have any voice that he was sure that Gary too would not want to go. Melody said that Lori had told them that the trip would only last 2 or 3 weeks, but she thought the journey might be extended longer. Extended like they'd be there until I came to get them. Melody was also worried about her new business of ferrying people to and from their anchored boats in the harbor. I assured the kids that at the end of 3 weeks if they did not return, I would send Dan for them or get them myself. Carolina would well take care of Melody's launch business until Melody returned. Two days later, Lori and the children were off to the Philippines. There were 7 of them, and I would send along with them Maria and 20 of her top men as security. Maria and two men would fly along commercially, the others sent by C-130. I had told Sam he was the man of the house, and he was to take care of the little ones. Several days later, I got word from Nilo that Lori and her group had safely arrived.

Christmas was here, the children, the five of them again had wrapping paper and gifts spread across the floors. Ant spending less and less time with Pearl became Sunshine's companion. We had kept Salinas's two favorite horses. Sunshine was attracted to the animals, so for Christmas, we got Sunshine a horse of her own. Sunshine hadn't ridden as yet, but she was emitted with joy over the gift. That Christmas, we also gave Sunshine her father's watch. She put it on, and it slid right off over her small hand. I told her we would have it adjusted, but she asked that it be kept just as it was. She put it back on and held her arm up, not to let the watch slide off.

Salinas's three were 4, 5, and 7. It was Michelle, Kelly and then Jac. Then there was Cat's Jim, he was now 5, and June's Kayla, she was also 5. The 5 of them could all swim like a fish and, of course, ride. We took the whaler and headed over to what I called Rusty's barbecue beach. Here the children watched as I dove and peaked under the rocks. Michelle was the only one that did what I did. Michelle caught her First crawfish! June was right there in the water with us. We all had a good time. June and Kayla got too much sun; the other children and I were what some people called tanned; we said we were brown.

Later that night, we called General Santos, but we didn't get through.

I had now spent two weeks with June, what a fine woman she turned out to be. Pearl didn't seem to like the attention I was giving June and privately expressed so. Pearl said that Lori left trying to get my attention and let me know what I had to lose. Pearl got in the

the computer more than I did and asked me about the three "new" C-130s that were being built? At this very moment, Pearl said, one of the three was being delivered to G.D.s Fairbanks facility. She looked bewildered when I said I knew nothing of the new C-130s and that they must belong to someone else.

I hadn't talked much to the new President of G.D., in fact I didn't have how to contact him but at the plant. I believed G.D. would be closed for the week due to the holidays. I thought it would be after New Years before I could reach him.

The next day Jerry called and said that our old friend, the Admiral, had contacted him; the Pentagon wanted to contract SCS to start moving equipment to a supply route to the Middle East. Jerry said his first trip would be to Saudi Arabia. Jerry said that Crowbe was also contacted for the same reason. Jerry said his first trip would be leaving the next day, December 27th. Jerry then asked about TESS? I sure would feel better knowing TESS was aboard, Jerry said. I then said that the G.D. Plant was most likely closed. But Jerry then said no way; the Admiral said that The Government had G.D. working overtime. Jerry said the plant was open. The first stage TESS unit's had little defense, only that 100 miles it messed with the Navigational and electrical systems. I would call the G.D. President and see what they could do and how fast.

My call was well received, and the G.D. President said that they could reinstall one of the two TESS units into Jerry's planes in a matter of hours. John was the G.D. President's name. I had not even met him. John then said that he was going to contact me today about an order they received. He said he received a message that the Saudi Government had purchased three new C-130s and that the first one had shown up on Christmas Day. I told him I knew nothing about the new planes. As my conversation was taking place, a knock on my office door sounded. It was Jack; he said it was necessary. I opened the door, and I put my hand over the phone's mouth part. Jack looked at me and said that a Saudi Royal C-130 had just landed at the airport, and there was a 737 from the same group to land behind it. I turned and looked at the computer and saw several messages had come in. I told John that Jerry would be sending his two planes and that I'd call him back. With Jack now in the office, I began to read. The first message was from Crown Prince Bihng that they requested a face-to-face meeting here on the Island. They'd be arriving today at 2:00 p.m. The second message was from the Admiral then one from the White House. The Admiral asked me to call him on a secure line; the White House message was an invitation.

I called the Admiral's office, he took the call, Captain he said, it's been too long. What exactly is going on Sir I asked? The Admiral then said, Son, the Soviet Union has officially closed down. The one possible country that could have backed Iraq has withdrawn. The Saudi Prince is on the way to visit you. He should be arriving at any moment. We didn't know in advance they were coming; we only figured out where they were headed an hour ago. While I was talking, Jack had sat at the computer. Jack was in contact with Dan, Jack put Dan on notice to alert that the Prince's 737 was in route and that it may have a military escort. Jack also passed the News of a New Russia.

The Admiral said that they had approved the Saudi's purchase of three new C-130s without hesitation. It was only when one landed at Fairbanks that we figured that they may have made some arraignments with you, he said. Our ambassador, the Admiral, stated, made direct contact and asked what their intentions were. We informed them that TESS units were not for sale. I said that I had no contact from anyone with regards to any C-130s nor TESS. The Admiral then said that our Government was against anyone or Government having access to TESS. I said that I would meet with the Saudi Prince and get back to him. I told the Admiral that based on how it went with the Prince; I would then decide about the White House visit.

I returned the message from the Saudis that we would receive the Prince here at Hill Top. The women folk were informed that they had little time to prepare for a Royal Visit. Angee would also be on-site doing some of her food specialties.

It was 2:00 P.M. sharp that the Prince and his people showed up at the house. The Prince looked to be about 30 years old. At first, there was no mention of why they came here. The Prince seemed interested in meeting the children and, of course, June. June didn't dress like a Bahamian, not a flower. Flowers were handed to the Prince. June wore a short white dress with a high collar and short sleeves. The Prince was well informed as he inquired about Lori and the other children. We had moved to the screened porch on the ocean side of the house, we were served up some crawfish fritters and of course, conch salad. Pearl had asked if she and Johnny could provide some entertainment, and I had warned the Prince ahead of time.

First, there was a low fly-by that the Prince and his people looked uncomfortable with. I then stepped out to the balcony with the Prince following. I had been expecting the T28s; what we got was a Harrier Jet. The second past was closer than a half-mile out over the water, with the Harrier flying at first upside down, then beginning to roll over and over. The next move was the most impressive. Pearl came around and hovered over the water then the jet start to spin like a top. Needless to say that I was impressed, but the Prince started clapping and didn't stop until the spinning slowly stopped. As the jet stopped, the front of the plane pointed at us and, yes, took a bow. From the bow, Pearl then pointed the Harrier at a 45 decrees up and, with a thrust of power, took off like the wind.

I could tell the Prince was impressed, he then said, that must be your daughter Pearl. It would help if you allowed Pearl to come to perform for the King, the Prince said. The King is not impressed easily, he said, but I'm sure he has not seen anything like that. Well, the Prince said, I have come to request your assistance. There soon will be small, and we trust short war to remove The Iraqis from Kuwait. Your President has assured our King that the war will not spread over into Saudi Arabia. We will participate in this war, and it is possible that Iran could take advantage of that situation and revive its war with Iraq. We do not want to cripple Iraq completely; we will remove them from Kuwait and send them back into Iraq. We want to hire your TESS to keep our kingdom from an air attack. Husain could easily send some of his many sud missiles into our lands.

We are expected to lose some of our military personnel, but our civilian population and cities must not be touched; the Kingdom must be protected.

The Prince went on to say that they had purchased three new C-130s; one is sitting at Fairbanks, the second will be ready in 30 days, and the third in 90 days from the second. The Prince then said we would make a gift of all three airplanes, pay all expenses plus a fair amount for your service. We would be eternally grateful.

The Prince then looked at June and said that he realized what they were asking and that if I agreed that it wouldn't be for the money. Our Land and families will come under attack; your husband could save thousands of lives. June looked at the Prince and said that she would stand by my decision but added that I had twice already flown important missions over there that had saved thousands, including from the terrible death of Husain's chemical gas factory. On one such trip, June stated, the captain's plane had landed on Saudi soil to restart an engine that had stalled from the percussion of an anti-aircraft gun, the second trip, his ride was shot down. June went on to say that the Captain's decision, if it were only to lose his life, would be easy for him; however, his decision could very well cost him something much dearer.

The Prince paused, then turned and clapped his hands; one of his people then brought up a small box. The Prince open the box and took out what looked like a small oil lamp, he first looked at June and as he spoke turned his head to me. You have both, of course, heard the old story's of a laden and his lamp; of course, you have, he said. No he then said this is not that lamp, this lamp was found at one of our most beautiful Oasis. As the Prince handed me the lamp he again reached into the box, looking at and holding the second item, the Prince said that they believed at one time there had been a settlement at the Oasis site. The lamp and bracelet are like no other. By the normal eyes these items are made from a shinny gold. Gold they are the Prince said. However, this gold is mixed with a material that makes these items almost unbreakable. One can not even scratch these items. These are a gift from our King. With it comes the offer to visit the site and share what you may find, perhaps a touch of the heavens.

When June saw the bracelet, her eyes widened; I was sure the Prince believed that June saw a rare beauty in the bracelet. What June noticed was that the bracelet that the Prince was handing her looked identical to the one that Pearl had come to us wearing, but Sunshine now wore. June looked at me and she knew that I too had notice the similarity in the two bracelets. For me, this Bracelet was the fourth, the one I had taken from the first Vehicle, the one that Victoria had worn, Pearl's that Sunshine now wore, and the gift from the Prince.

The Prince, still standing, said, I will go now and let you think about this. If you don't mind, I said, I'll ride along with you back to your plane. Yes the Prince said, please do. June thanked the Prince for the gifts. The Prince looking back at June said that I was a very lucky man.

On our way to the airport, I inquired about the Prince's cousin Prince Rashid. Rashid was, of course, the man that had taken and married Martha. The Prince was not pleased with my question; I found it wasn't my question but the name Rashid. Rashid, the Prince said, is not of my blood. Rashid's father was a friend and servant of my father. Rashid's father passed away, leaving the fortune that my father bestowed upon him to his many sons. The oldest living son is a radical that has been expelled from the Kingdom. Rashid is of the youngest and pledged his allegiance to the elder brother. If your friend's daughter is married to Rashid, may Ala be merciful on her.

The Prince then returned to the conversation at hand; he looked at me and said that a man must do what a man was born to do. A man he said doesn't let women interfere with what he must do. You Captain, the Prince said are a warrior. You are certainly no Judas but also not one of the other 11 disciples. Yes, the Prince said with a smile, we have heard many stories of your fishing adventures. The King's brother had the pleasure to meet and fish with your Catherine on the Nassau Queen. My uncle, the Prince said, has fond memories of his fishing trip. The Prince then said we would have to sit together soon and trade stories. The limo stopped, the doors opened, and the Prince took my hand and said he knew we would see each other soon.

The Prince was aboard his 737, and my car was waiting with a pleasant surprise; Pearl and Johnny had returned from Paix; Pearl said she wanted to get a better look at the Prince. Pearl and Johnny had flown Pearl's T28 back from Paix. I didn't mention anything to Pearl about the bracelet; I wanted to be sure of what I was thinking before speaking.

While gone, June had compared the two bracelets, her then seeing that the two were identical. June said she was careful not to mix them and had put both gifts in our safe in the master bedroom. June said that Sunshine when seeing the second bracelet, asked if we had also located her mother's bracelet? June, as she quite often did, thought as I did that maybe one of the fishermen that had found Sunshine had noticed and kept the two bracelets of Sunshine's mother's and Sunshine's.

When returning to Hill Top, June confirmed that the two braces were the same and mentioned what she had thought about maybe there were at least two more bracelets out there. I told June what the old man that had found Sunshine said about selling the jewelry that was taken from the dead. June asked what I would do and how I planned to break the news to Lori?

Since Lori had gone, we had only heard from Maria and Nilo. Lori had now been gone two weeks; I had promised Melody and Sam that if they hadn't returned by the third week, I would come to fetch them. There was also the White House invitation. If we were going to do this thing, I would need to hear what the President had to say.

I sent the message to both Lori and Maria that I needed to speak with Lori. I then answered the White House invitation saying that I could be there tomorrow morning. I then called the Admiral and let him know what was going on. I then called John of G.D. and told him that I would be there either tomorrow or or the following day. John asked what they would do with the new C-130, and I advised that it was on hold.

My decision was made. However, I wanted Lori to hear it from me before from others.

Not hearing back as yet from the White House nor General Santos, early the next morning June and I rode over to Andros to check by chance if the old man or someone remembered the Bracelets. June would ware the Bracelet from the Prince, this to perhaps have it recognized by the old man or someone on the island.

June and I traveled to Andros via Donzi, the weather was good, and we anchored about 100 feet off the beach at the fishing village. June and I swam in alone, this not to worry the villagers with our security. As we walked out of the water, a wave caught us both by surprise, and we both rolled up onto the beach. As I gave a hand to help her up, I saw this beautiful woman rising to her feet. I embraced her and kissed her as I had not in several years. June was wearing a small blouse over her bathing suit top and of course the gold bracelet. We both had swum to shore, holding a pair of Sandals for the hot sand. I of course, wore a small waterproof pouch that carried my stainless Walter and was wearing my American speedo. June took my hand and we walked to the old man's house from whom we had purchased the Commander's watch. The old man was helpful with information saying that yes he remembered the bracelets and two special rings. He said that the two rings would be hard to forget due to the Nazi symbol on the face of the rings. I remember, the fisherman said, that I got the watch and my two brothers the bracelets, my brothers are now both gone, they were both heavy drinkers, that's why I say they must have sold the bracelets. Only one other fisherman from that trip was still live; he may remember something of the other jewelry. We walked about a half mile to find a feeble old man that didn't seem to know what was going on. His family there said the old man had lost his mind and would be of no help. In the sand I drew the Nazi sign, the old man looked at it and turned and entered his small room. The old man returned with a ring saying that no one wanted to buy it, so he had kept it. The ring was gold with a black stone with the Nazi symbol set in the gold. The ring also had writing on the inside of which I couldn't quite make out.

I would like to buy the ring from you old man, I said. He looked at me, asking why I wanted it. I told him that I was a collector. It must then have some value, he said. I looked at at family member that had told us that the old man had lost his mind and said, pretty smart. The old man then said $1,000. I opened my pouch and counted out 10, 100 dollar bills. We then turned our attention to the bracelet that June was wearing. The old man then shook his head, saying he didn't remember the Bracelet. A family member said that they had remembered that the bar owner had brought some of the jewelry for his wife. He wasn't sure, but it could have been a bracelet. We thanked the old man and family members. The original old fisherman walked us back to the beachside, where I added another $100 for his help. I told the old man that if he remembered anything more or located the bracelets, then he should contact the hotel owners, and they would contact us. Of course, we will pay you well for your time.

June and I dropped off our sandals and walked into the water. The ring must have been for a small man as it only fit onto my pinky finger. Once at the Donzi, we were helped into the boat. The anchor was pulled, the boat's motor started and zoom; we were off and heading to the channel. We powered through the channel and on into the swells of the TOTO.

Two hours later, we were entering Nassau's Harbor.

With the wind and waves, there was nothing June, and I could have talked about during the ride back. At home, we went straight to the office to check messages. Maria had responded saying that Lori had said that whatever conversation we would have would be in General Santos.

The White House responded that the President would be at Camp David and would like me to visit him there. I would leave within the next hour. While June got my things together, she asked my thoughts about at least two Nazis being with the Commander at his death? I said that we may never know but that the "Fortuna" had just visited Cuba. Batista was then the present dictator that had the year before overthrown Prio. Batista was President of Cuba during most of World War Two and could have had contact with the Nazis, even Hitler himself. If Hover had known all the facts, Hover and his men could have thought they needed to step right in. We didn't know how close the Commander was to having his lasers a working weapon. Remember I said it was the U.S. that had killed the Commander's father. Maybe the Commander was working with the other side. I stopped and took the ring into a better light and used a magnifying glass. The ring was dated 1933 with a name of whom I did not know; hell, I thought that the Nazis hadn't got started until 1939. I wouldn't be taking or mentioning the ring in Maryland.

Jerry would send one of his men to Andros to continue searching for the two bracelets and maybe the other Nazi ring.

My trip north to Camp David went as well as could be expected. The President knew all about the Saudi offer and did not oppose it just as long as he could have at least two of his people aboard the C-130s at all times. I did not oppose this but I knew then that the President didn't trust me just to let his people in. He would be watching our every move. The President didn't mention Sunshine; it was as if he hadn't been aware of her presents. Maybe it was as it seemed, the Navy thinking Sunshine only had several disabilities. Sunshine not speaking, and her odd look could have had her locked away but also it could have saved her life. Indeed whoever had the Commander killed wouldn't have let her live.

I hadn't seen the President since before the Noriega thing, and he didn't bring it up. The end of the short meeting would open the doors required to proceed with our plan. The President said they'd hold back until we had at least two C-130s in the air. The President never directly mentioned their pending military action, but I got the message. The President was right assuming that I had decided to do this, as by now, things were in the works.

From Maryland I flew to Fairbanks, my security as well as Fairbanks's was high. John was aware of the dangers working with me brought to the table. I carried in the two older TESS units; Jerry had not one but both of his C-130 already at the plant. Fairbanks looked like a C-130 parking lot. John's and my meeting would be privet; he was surprised by my request but agreed it would be the easiest and fastest way to get the New C-130 on its way. Us not providing the details of our plan could catch the President's men off guard. Of course the new C-130 and Jerry's planes would need to be checked for any GPS and or government bugs.

While there, we also agreed on a purchase for four of our now improved laser cannons. Paix was now equipped with six such lasers, and even Hill Top had a miniature version.

I had carried eight men with me and left six at the plant. These six men were to live at the plant. They would do two men 12 hours, 8:00 a.m. to 8:00 p.m, the next two men 8:00 p.m. until 8:00 a.m. with two men off two days. These shifts would be two days at a time. The rules, no weapons abroad but ours, no photos and nothing was to leave the plane. One man aboard, one man on the ground.

Supposedly I was now again on the Government good guy list. I would now fly down to Miami and meet with Lourdes and Evette. Lourdes again divorced, and Evette was again working for Omni. I had also called home asking June to meet me at the Sonora hotel on Key Biscayne. I was anxious to walk down the beach with June to revisit the lighthouse at the end of the Key.

My meeting with Lourdes and Evette was to asked if they were still free to work, travel and make some big money? Both ladies were ready and willing. Lourdes's children were now at the age where their grandmother would do taking care of them. Lourdes was ok with the possibility of a long skirt and head ware while Evette wasn't. Evette asked how she was to catch some rich Arab if they couldn't see me? Both girls knew that Lori had gone to General Santos, but nighter knew what was happening with Lori and me; hell, I didn't even know.

Evette was to head to Limon and shut down our operation there, pulling all 26 of our personnel out of Nicaragua. Joel would be the only one that would stay in Limon, keeping his ears to the ground. It had now been a year since the Sandinista lost in a countrywide election. Things were going good; most of the Contras had now returned to their farming. Most, the ones that lived were better off than they were before the war. Managua now had uninterrupted lights and water. The harbors had been cleared of mines, and the Fruit companies were talking about going back. Many prominent families had either moved to Spain or Miami.

June showed up at the Hotel, we dressed, and we visited Joe's Stone Crab on the beach. Man were those stone crabs good. From Joe's, we went to see the movie, Dancing With Wolves, June said, that in a way the movie reminded her of us. From the movie, it was back to the Hotel.

For me, the meaning of a great hot shower hadn't changed; it was just that it hadn't happened in a while. Tonight my, our shower was great.

The next morning June and I were up early and out for a jog. We headed down to the lighthouse. June and I had sailed over here several times when we were dating in high school. The lighthouse had since been remodeled; the area was no longer called Crandon Park, the Zoo had been moved to somewhere in South Miami, and the roller rink, well it too, was gone.

On the way back, it rained, it being the beginning of winter, the rain was cold, we entered the water, as the water was much warmer than the cool rain. There are no waves on this part of the beach, not far out was a sand bar that blocked any small waves that would have been. It rained for almost 30 minutes. I almost had wished it not to stop, but it did.

Tomorrow would be two years since the passing of Montibelli; Christmas was Lori's and my wedding anniversary. June said things happen for a reason.

I would spend New Year at Hill Top, then head to General Santos. Jack would be in charge of what we called Home Security while Dan would be in charge of the C-130 projects. So far only John from G.D. and I knew that I had authorized that the original computer from the first Vehicle be placed in the newest C-130. I would keep the new C-130 at Paix and send our Paix number one to Saudi Arabia. This way, there would be much less chance of losing the original computer. I hoped with G.D. doing this, we could catch the President's men off guard, flying the new plane to Paxi and making the switch without any notice.

I would be landing in General Santos without any notice to Lori. Maria would know and be ready to leave as Maria would be used in our upcoming Saudi operations. I brought with me the number one man in charge of Paix. He in turn brought with him six men of his pick. I would fly out with Melody, Sam, Maria, and six men.

Maria met us at the General Santos airport and I was delivered to the shrimp and fish packing plant. Lori was there working in the plant; Lori was wearing high top rubber boots, long rubber gloves, and a hair net. Seeing her like that reminded me of the first time she had caught my eyes down on the fishing dock. This time she really did have two children of her own. Six years had gone by just like that. Lori didn't see me at first; then, I let out a whistle that got her attention. Lori smiled and came a running. As Lori reached me, she jumped into my arms; before kissing me, she said, it's for real. Before my kiss ended I had two more hugging me. It was Melody and Sam; both had been working with Lori.

Melody said she knew I would come for them. Lori wanted to show me how the plant was working; we, she said, are shipping two frozen shrimp containers per week. We are also doing well with frozen fish. Lori was proud of the work they were doing and bragged about how Melody and Sam were contributing to the plant. I asked Lori if she would go to the house with me to see Gary and Joe-Anne, and she said she would need to finish her shift. Melody looked at me and said to please not leave without her.

I again kissed Lori and was on my way to the house. This house, of course, was called the Santos house. It was here in the house of Mrs. Santos that Lori and I had been married. Mrs. Santos had passed away within hours of our wedding.

It was great to see Gary and Joe-Anne; they were getting so big. There also at the House was, of course, Chubby and Lilly. Mia and her little girl were also there; Mia had another big belly; Mia said this time it was a boy. Malcolm, Mia said, was working on a particular project in the Banana packing house. The house looked busy with people coming and going. Nilo had finally caught up with me. It was good to see him. Nilo asked how long I planned to stay? I smiled and said the Leer would not leave without me being aboard. Nilo said he was afraid of that. Nilo said that Crowlbe had rehired the two older Strider Class row-row ships we had initially started with. Nilo was afraid that we would soon be leaving cargo behind.

We are doing well Nilo said but we are still last on the totem poll. I asked where Nilo had gotten that expression from; Nilo said he got that from Malcolm.

Nilo said we would still have our agreed slots, but now we were shipping almost 45 containers a week. Forty-five containers a week, I repeated. With a big smile, Nilo said, yes, Captain 45 per week. My friend still doing good, I asked? Nilo said that the old masked man was now the General Santos Mayor and running for the provincial Governorship. He has been asking for you, Nilo said. And the clinics and the schools I asked? All good, Nilo said. And the restaurant, I asked? We have a full house at lunch almost every day. That's great I said; any problems, I asked? Nilo hesitated and said only one, Lori, he said. What about Lori, I asked? Again Nilo hesitated. Spit it out, man, I said. Lori said she would not leave here, he said. She has told the workers that she will stay and raise her family here. I looked at Maria and Maria said that it was true. And the children, I asked? Maria said that Lori said you would not take them from her. Sam, Maria said will also stay. Lori has said that you have not been tired from the fight and maybe never will.

I would have liked to grabbed up the children and left that very moment. I did not.

When Lori got home she looked tired, but not to tired to hold both of our children in her arms. Then, of course, there was me. I got and enjoyed a good shower. I was sure she wanted me to remember it.

Lori said she was still in love with me and always would be, but she said she was staying put. No more guns in the house, no more sleepless nights worrying whether I would be coming home or not. On this trip, Lori had heard the story of me being the last person to meet with the Philippine Colonel before he had a heart attack and ran his car into a tree. Lori had been told by Salinas about the time that the Police Chief from Mandeville had some kind of attack while attempting to have Salinas's horses taken from her. Lori was sure that the Philippine Colonel's death was my Revenge for the death of Lieutenant Joe-Anne.

Lori said that Pearl no longer needed her, as Pearl was now like me on an adventure that kept her away from the house for days at a time. That too Lori said, could end in tragedy. Lori then said it all; you promised that one day this house and all the businesses here would all be mine. Come live here with us Lori said. It's yours too. I asked what she had planned for the lack of ship's space that was coming soon? Lori said she would need some financial assistance but would build at least one ship of her own and order more equipment. Lori said that Malcolm was experimenting with nitrogen and that once in a refrigerated container, adding nitrogen would stop the fruit ripening for 90 days. This could enable us to have our own ship call here twice a month she said. We are now shipping 90 TEUs per week, she said. The new acreage that I purchased three years ago now has bananas and pineapples on it, she said. Soon our shipping needs will almost double. Lori said that she would travel to China and Russia to open new markets.

It all sounds good, I said; I will pick up Gary and Joe-Anne at the beginning of the summer. June first, and have them back three months later. If this is agreeable, I will deed you everything now except the original Santos house, its land, the fish factory, and adjoining property. The house will be set in trust for Gary and the Fish Factory for Joe-Anne. I will want half of the first ten years of profit to be put in trust for Melody, Sam, Gary and Joe-Anne. I will lend you money with your assets as a guarantee.

Do you agree I asked? Lori said yes.

I did not kiss her again, I walked to the bedroom door and walked down the stairs. Melody was downstairs waiting with Sam.

I hugged Sam and asked if he was staying? Sam said he would stay to take care of Lori and the children. I told him that I would be here on June first to pick up the children, and I'd be happy if he wanted to come along with them. Chubby and Lilly said they would also stay with Lori. Lilly said that little Gary and Joe-Anne were their only grandchildren. I looked at them and said that I understood.

I looked at Melody and said we were leaving in the morning.

Both Gary and Joe-Anne were now in bed, and I went and got in the bed with Gary.

The following day we were headed to the airport when flagged down by three cars, Malcolm, Nilo, and the Mayor. All wanted to chat and say good by.

I wasn't a bit happy about leaving Lori and especially the children. June first would be here before I knew it, and if the children didn't want to go back at the end of August, I would not send them back.

Dan was now located at the G.D. Plant; Jerry's two C-130s had already flown out. Dan sent a computer message that the New C-130 was test flown. Dan said that TESS was performing as expected. Dan said he figured another two days. This, Dan said, was no cargo plane. Back in Paxi, our number One Bird was being readied to leave for Saudi Arabia. The Prince had been notified that we would be visiting within the week.

The trip home was longer than the one going; I believed this because I didn't feel right about what took place with Lori and leaving the children.

June wasn't surprised with the Lori news; June made it clear that this didn't give me the all-clear to be looking for a replacement.

Pearl was at the house and said that she would have Lori build her a concrete slab that she could land her Harrier on to visit her and the children. Pearl said she would miss seeing Sam most of all. I asked about refueling, and Pearl said she was working on it.

Jerry wrote that hundreds if not thousands of Nazis had escaped from Germany at the war's end. Jerry noted that even the U.S. had relocated some of them. Jerry said that the Nazis might have been here working with the Commander on his laser project. It got me thinking that maybe it wasn't the Commander they, whomever they were, were after. If that was the case, the Israelis should also be added to the list of suspects for the Commander's murder.

Somehow the news about Lori traveled very quickly. I supposed the information came from Melody; it wasn't a secret.

Two days passed, and Dan showed up at Paix with the New C-130. The new bird would be put on stand by while Dan would head the Saudi project, as we would call it. Dan would also get two new helicopters that would be used for his support. Jack would now take on all the home security on a full-time basis. Cindy disapproved of Lori's actions but said that she would need Jack close to home. June, Jack, and Dan wanted to know where this put me. I said that unless things started to heat up before, I would be close by home until the next C-130 was ready. If things heated up first, I'd take the number two Bird and head that way. Jack and I had made a date one week from today to do a trial run with the New C-130.

Today I would get dropped of at the Chalks airline dock and hop a Seaplane to Miami. My passport was expiring, which gave me an excuse to get gone.

CHAPTER XI

MIAMI

THE FLIGHT STILL LEFT PARADISE Island at 3:30 p.m. and arrived at Watson Island in Miami at 4:30 p.m.

From Watson Island, I'd catch a cab to the 1800 Club. It had been some time since I visited the Club. It was early for Jan or Billy to be there; today, I was just another customer. The only thing the same was that my old seat at the club was empty.

From the club, I would visit the sailing club. Paul wasn't there; it was a young lady behind the bar; she looked like she was still in high school. I asked about Paul, and the girl said that Paul had gone back to school and that he had an exam he was studying for. The girl introduced herself as Kay. I said my name was JP. It was strange, I didn't recognize anyone at the bar, and they didn't recognize me. Kay asked if I had a sailboat here, and I said mine was a 38 foot Morgan. From behind me, a man asked if I was the owner of the "Lori"? I spun around in my stool and, looking at the man, said, yes, Sir. The man said that his son was the one that was keeping the batteries up and the bottom clean. A bit surprised, I asked if I owed his son any money? The man then said, oh no, his son was paid up. Well then, I said, please tell him that I appreciate his hard work. Kay then quickly asked if I was going to take the sailboat out tonight? Well, I said I hadn't planned on it, but now that I know that the batteries are good and the bottom clean, I might take her out for a sail. You a good night sailor that same man asked? My son says your boat has about a 4-foot draft. I again spun around and said that I had been sailing the bay for more than 30 years. Don't see you at the Club that much the man said. Yes, Sir, I said I live in Nassau. Then Kay, at my back, said, you must be Captain Jim. Swinging back around, I said yes, mam, and how you might know about Captain Jim. Kay then said that she used to babysit for Penny and Paul, their son; Kay said, their son is named after you. Penny and Paul always were telling stories about you, she said. Kay said that Paul still tells the story of the night you were in here as a boy telling him about the big shark and the biggest crawfish you ever caught. Kay then turned and up from the wall; she took down a framed photo I had given Paul. Kay handed me the photo; I took it in my hands, staring at it; tears began to slide down my cheeks. Here in my hands was the photo of Johnny, Rusty, and myself holding that big 4 foot crawfish that I had regrettably speared on my first trip to the Bahamas. Kay took the photo and looked at it, and said, Yes, it's you alright. The man that had been behind me was now standing at my shoulders, asking to see the photo. Kay handed the man the photo, and with the man looking at the picture, he said that Paul had told the story 100 times. The man then turned and said, hey guys, this is the boy that Paul always talks about. The man looked at me and said his name was Gil. Others also introduced themselves. One such man said that my Uncle's photo was on their wall as one of the first Commodores of the Club. Gil asked to buy me a beer, as I looked Kay was digging in the cooler and pulled out a Saint Pauli Girl. This beer Kay said, is always at the bottom of the cooler. Kay said that Paul always says he has these just in case you stop by. Kay put the beer on the counter and opened it. I then said that this was the beer that my old friend Mr. Brown had served Rusty and me at the city dock bar in Nassau. Rusty and I were 15 years old back then I said. Rusty, I said, is the blond kid in the photo. Then Gil noted that Paul said that you had a 12-foot hammerhead shark for a pet. That caused some laughter. I said that no one owned that shark. He could have eaten me and I could have eaten him, I said. That shark came up on me without me seeing him until his big head was within arm's reach; his left eye looked right at me as it passed. The sharks tail almost pushed me aside as it swam by. Yeh and how'd you save him, one man asked? Several months later we caught that shark on a night line. We used the crawfish trap winch to pull him in. When we got his head up to the boat, I was ready to pound his head with my bat; I saw that big eye looking at me and stopped. I then cut the line, and he was again free. Kay then took the photo and rehung it on the back wall. Paul, she said, would be sorry he missed you. Kay then turned and reached for the phone. Don't call him, I said, let him study. She turned back and asked how long I would be In town? I said that I was here in Miami only for the day but that if Paul worked tomorrow night that I would stop by if at all possible. Another man in the bar asked what kind of work I did in Nassau? I said we were in the Crawfish and Tourist business. What do you do for the Tourist? He asked? We take them fishing, and if their real adventurous, they can see a real treasure ship. You find any treasure down there one man asked? Some I said. Then for the first time, I looked at Kay; she reminded me of June so many years ago.

Well, I said, if I'm going to get that sail, I'd better get going. I said I'd bring the Morgan around the dock and if she was closing up before I got her alongside, for Kay to leave a hoagie and a six-pack of coke in the icebox outside. I asked for my tab to include the sandwich and cokes. I thanked Kay for the memories and left a 100 dollar bill on the bar.

I didn't see a night time dock master, so I got in one of several rowboats and headed out. I arrived at the boat and tied the row boat at the stern. I reached inside the top of my shirt and took off a small gold chain holding keys from around my neck. I opened the hatch door and felt for the lights. With the engine room lit. I checked the oil. It looked new and was right on the full line.

From the cockpit, I turned the blower on, waited 30 seconds, then turned the key. The engine started and sounded good. As the engine ran, I walked up the side to the bow and unhooked the mooring from it's cleat. The mooring line went over and only the mooring float could then be seen. I walked back to the stern and got behind the wheel, and put her in gear. There wasn't much space between boats; it seemed that the sailing club had grown. As I came up to the dock, I put the engine in reverse, neutral, and shut her down. The boat's bow stopped right at the dock. I stepped off with the bow line and a port stern line. I tied the bow line and then, walking back to the stern, pulled in the stern and tied her off. I then got back aboard and got the rowboat line, and jumped in to tie her back with the others. I then went back aboard and looked for some clothes to change into. My clothes were there mixed in with some of Lori's. While up in the small stateroom, I also grabbed a pair of Lori's shorts and a bathing suit top, and one of my shirts. I changed clothes and laid Lori's clothes on the bunk.

As I came up from the cabin, there she was, standing on the dock. It, of course, was Kay asking if I wanted company? I won't be returning tonight, I said. Kay then said her first class started at 10:00 a.m. tomorrow. Will you be back before then she asked? I looked down at her feet and there was two hoagie's a six-pack of coke, and a bag of ice. All packed, I see. Yes Sir she said. Did you call your mom to let her know? Kay said that she called her mom to let her know she was staying with a friend. Are you sure I asked? I'm a good swimmer, she said. Come aboard I said. She handed me the food, drinks, and ice, and I took her hand as she stepped over the port cable railing. I said there were some clothes in the front cabin. I then started the engine, stepped on the dock, unhooked the stern line throwing it aboard. I then walked to the bow line, unhooking it, stepping aboard with the line. I walked to the stern behind the wheel and put her in gear. The boat was 100 feet from the dock when Kay came up from the cabin. You set these clothes out for someone, she asked? I see they fit, I said. The shirt is a bit big she said. You sail I asked? I took pram lessors here at the Club, she said. Me too I said. It was a few years back but, me too. We motored out the channel, the wind was from the north, north east. I picked out a compass heading and showed her how to keep the heading. I could tell she got it. With the new heading we were heading into the wind. As I walked up to the bow, I unhooked the mainsail from the tie backs that were holding it wrapped around the boom; from the bow, I raised the sail. I walked back to the cockpit and pulled in the jib line. I then took the wheel and made a heading for the sand bank channel markers. Once we had a new heading with the compass. I gave the wheel back to Kay while I went below. Below I turned out all the lights besides the running lights and the compass. I then took the keys that were again around my neck and unlocked the gun cabinet. I wasn't thinking I was going to need anything; it was just habit. Once in the cockpit I again took the wheel and turned off the engine. Now the only sound was the wind and the small wake of the boat. Kay standing at my side, asked how I knew? Knew what I asked? I would be coming with you, she asked? I didn't know, but I did want you to come. Do you always get what you want Kay asked? No, mam, not at all, but if those clothes weren't there, then you wouldn't have known that I was interested in you coming along. Kay said that Paul had told her that you always either came with a girl or one came looking for you. Kay said that Paul said that you had been married at least twice.

Well, I said this time I came by myself, and my last wife left me. Not for another man, Kay asked? No I said, she said it was either her or the adventure. Kay said that the adventure must have won out.

We were about two miles from the channel markers when my buzzer started going off, then the cell phone. My cell was on my hip belt that held my gun pouch. I opened my pouch and put in an earplug. Dan said that two copters had taken off heading my way, one from Fort Lauderdale which had an ETA of 6 minutes the other much closer coming from Tamiami. That copter was only 3 minutes away.

I changed the boat's heading more to the east and tightened both the main sail and jib. I told Kay to hold that course. I then went down and brought up two rifles, a tubular box, and a jacket. I helped Kay put on the jacket then picked up the 30-06; Dan said he was on the way but would be too late to stop the first copter. With the new heading, I could now see the first copter's spotlight. I took aim and fired. With the spotlight not going out, I again aimed and fired. This time the spot light went out. I then put down the 30-06 and picked up the M16; I had two forty-round clips tapped together. As the copter got closer, I let off the first clip's 40 rounds. The copter pulled up and passed us on our stern. As I changed clips, the copter pointed upward and started making a 360-degree turn. As the copter came around, it was struck by a rocket that came from the southeast. The copter exploded and went down in pieces. I then put down the M16 and again picked up the 30-06. As I spotted the second copter's light and took aim, the second copter exploded as did the first; a fighter jet swooped over the wreckage and hovered, then turned and flew into the darkness. With my phone piece still in, I said loudly, Pearl I told you that Harrier couldn't be armed. It wasn't long before we heard the roar of the C-130. Dan then said that all systems were showing clear and they would be moving back.

By now, I had got a look at Kay; she was trembling a bit. Almost in complete shock, she asked if this was some kind of a show, it wasn't real right? The burnt smell from the second copter had just reached us. Kay said it smelled like fireworks. I looked at her, saying that it was the performance of a lifetime. Still wide-eyed, Kay asked if the jacked was Kevlar? I then said that she could now remove the vest and yes it was. As I reached for the large zipper, Kay took and stopped my hand and said she'd keep it on.

Our position of the boat and the wind now had us going through the channel. We sailed another 4 miles and headed into one of Sand's Keys coves. I had Kay head into the wind; it wasn't much as we were in the lee of the Island. I dropped the main sail and anchor. I walked to the cockpit and then rolled up the jib. Now there was not a sound to be heard. Getting back to the cockpit, Kay asked if we were safe here? I stepped to her and I sipped down the vest's zipper. I removed the vest and unbuttoned my shirt. I looked at her and asked if she was alright. Kay then said, it was real wasn't it? I said yes then kissed her.

The next morning I was up early doing chores. For the second time this morning, I pulled up anchor and raised the main. The boat turned to the starboard when I wanted it to turn to port. When stepping down into the cockpit I turned the wheel, and we jibed with the boom quickly passing as I ducked my head as it passed. The bow was now pointing west north west, I tightened the main then let out the jib, hooking it through the cleat and winding in the jibe tight. The boat heeled to port, and we were on our way. The jib must have woken Kay; Kay then came upon the cockpit's deck to kiss me good morning. After my kiss, Kay said that after last night she would never be the same. Kay said that when she left the dock with me the night before, she thought the worst that could happen to us was to run aground.

As we went back through the channel returning home, Kay came up with the two hoagie's and two cold cokes.

Before reaching the sailing club, I dropped Kay off at the Dinner key Marina. I had given her money for a cab. We had agreed that if she was questioned, she was to call Lourdes before talking. I did not want her to lie about last night, only tell what she saw. Two helicopters exploding in the sky. Kay had asked if and when she might see me again?

Didn't scare you off, I asked? Kay said that no one she knew actually had any idea what real excitement was like. Again she asked me if it all had really happened?

As I came into the sailing club, I spotted my mooring float and went up on the bow and grabbed it as I passed by. I hooked it to the bow cleat then lowered the main, and rolled it up. I then rolled up the jib and locked down the cabin. I looked up and saw my old friend Robert. Yes Sir Robert said, I knew it was you just as soon as I saw them there police cars. I's didn't tell anyone about miss Kay's car still being here. She is alright, isn't she? Robert asked? In school by now I recon, I said. I jumped aboard, and Robert said there was a host of people waiting for me. On the dock was Lourdes and four of my men, Big Ted and two officers plus some un- friendly-looking faces.

As I got off the launch, Lourdes handed me a note that I read, then rolled it into a ball and gave one back to her. Lourdes asked if I was alright? I said, yes of course. Then there was Big Ted, we shook hands, and he asked if a pair of homicide detectives could search my boat. Of course, I said, they do have a search warrant, don't they? The smart detective said that one was on the way. Until then, I said; I then asked if maybe it was about those two explosions I had seen last night in the sky. How close were they to you, the detective asked? Well, it was hard to tell, I said; I had just gone through the channel at the old lighthouse on my way out to the ocean. It looked maybe five miles I said. You were alone, the other man asked? Yes, I said, I sailed all night, and I'm pretty tired. Your not interested in what brought the helicopters down, one man asked? Truthfully, I said, I didn't think much of it, I didn't know it was copters. I thought it was fireworks. Any one get hurt I asked? Ted then said that so far there were no survivors nor did they know whom was aboard or for that matter, whom the owners of the helicopters were. Well gentlemen I said I have my people here waiting for me; as I walked to the parking lot, the one detective stopped Lourdes and asked for the note that she had given me, Lourdes then looked at me, and said no. It's ok I said give it to them. Lourdes reached into her pocket and pulled out a ball of paper. Lourdes handed it to the Detective; he then held it in his hand and said we would be hearing from them.

The detective would see nothing but a note with the name and phone number of one of the girls that worked at the 1800 club. I had passed the original note to Ted when we shook hands.

I also wasn't worried what they might find on the boat. Early that morning, I had pulled up anchor and let out the jib to carry us closer to shore. It was about high tide and I rolled up the jib and dropped anchor before running aground. I went overboard and took the used shells and weapons to the edge of the mangroves. All the shells went as far into the mangrove as I could throw them, both rifles had been disassembled and I pushed the parts up into the bottom of the mangroves just as far as I could. I had opened the tube and pulled out the stinger that it housed. I twisted off the rocket part, the salt water entered into both the war head and the thruster. This, too, I pushed up into the mangroves. I was standing at high tide in three feet of water. All would be rusted away within months. Even if they were found someday, I had no attachment to any of the armaments.

Lourdes delivered me to the passport office, I still needed to renew my passport. From the passport office Lourdes dropped me off at the Opa Locka Airport, where none other than Tommy was waiting. As I exited the car, Lourdes said she and Evette would be in Paxi in two days. As I entered the Leer, Tommy had a comment about not being as young as we used to be. I looked his way and with a smile and said, speak for yourself.

Once in the Leer I got to the computer and sent a message to Jerry with what Little I knew of Kay and for him to find out the rest. I wanted to know everything I possibly could. Jerry was also on top of finding who was behind the copter attack and from whom the information came to them that I was out there sailing that night. Someone could have made me at the 1800 Club, but I didn't think so.

CHAPTER XII

OUR FRIST C-130 ARRIVES AT SAUDI ARABIA

DAN HAD MADE HIS WAY to Saudi Arabia, contacting the Prince and their Sky Marshall. Dan's group was given a small airport of their own near the border with Iraq. Dan took with him two sets of Pilots, mechanics, spares for everything, twenty of our Black Devils plus two Laser batteries that would protect our group on the ground that included the C-130. The setup there would also include Evette once there working on the communications.

The production of the second new C-130 had been moved up. G.D. said they were within days of having a New TESS ready. Looked like we were still at least two weeks off. The Admiral had contacted us and offered up two of their C-130s to help speed us getting into the air, but we would not take his offer.

It was now January 16th, like one of my favorite T-shirts says, "SHIT HAPPENS," on that same day, it looked like the war was getting ready to start. Someone had moved the war up without waiting. Our small base at the Saudi-Iraq border was attacked by a group of Iraqi regulars from the ground, Suds and fighter jets by air; only one Laser battery was up and working. At the time of the attack, the Saudi's were still in charge of security. The laser battery that was up and ready had picked up the Suds and alerted the pilots to get the C-130 off the ground. The laser battery knocked down two Suds before the C-130 could get in the air. Once in the air, TESS worked with the laser battery, knocking down the inbound Missiles plus four of Husain's fighter jets. There was no warning from any U.S. intel. The attack was repelled, however, not before losing four men, the hanger, most of our parts, and the ground computers. Something stunk about the whole thing. It was as if someone besides the Iraqis wanted us to fail. Dan had only been there two days.

Evette and Lourdes were waken from their sleep, and told that they must be on their way to Paxi by 8 a.m. this morning.

Our number two bird would be loaded and departing at 3:00 p.m., myself included. I had my last night at Hill Top and would leave for Paxi at 5:00 a.m. Jack would be in Paxi, as now only the first new C-130 would be left to protect Paxi and Nassau. Of course, we had a new weapon that already had been tested the night before.

I hadn't even known, but we now had two ex-marine Harrier pilots. Yes, the Harrier was traveling with us. Pearl wanted to go with us, but I told her she was needed here. The thought about what Lori had said about Pearl's involvement did enter my mind.

Before we all arrived in Paxi, Jack had the new C-130 up in the air testing doing his morning routine. Jack didn't meet us on the ground; Maria was now in charge of the loading of supplies, another two mechanics and six of her specially self-trained Black Devils. Maria said the best defense was a good offense. Maria said that Husain would be sorry he ever messed with her Black Devils.

It was good to see Evette, she looked better than I remembered. Lourdes would say behind at Paxi, Evette was in for the job of her life.

We took off that afternoon. The Israelis would be doing the refueling. The Saudi's were already putting up some temporary living quarters and had started rebuilding the hanger. Storage containers were brought in to use for our new supplies. While on the way, the war started. We were guided in by Dan; he was up in the air in our number one. We had flown in from the Israeli side into Saudi Arabia. We landed and were unloaded at once. Evette's communications room was ready within hours. I flew my first mission just 6 hours after arriving. Dan and his crew got their first rest in over 48 hours. The rules of engagement were clear; all aircraft were to stay at least a buffer of 100 miles from the territory we were to cover. When we moved, that buffer also moved. We would engage all aircraft in our zone. It wasn't, please get out of our zone, it was, one warning, then TESS would do it's thing. That first night, Dan knocked down six enemy aircraft. Any patrols that crossed into Saudi ground space were also warned then attacked. Our first use of the number two was without us trading shots with anyone. Dan was up in the air as we landed. Dan had met with Maria and approved Maria's plan. Maria and several of her Black Devils would go up with us on our second run. We would enter Iraq's territory, and Maria would parachute out about 20 miles into the Iraqis side. Maria and her Black Devils would hike back, engaging anyone that was between her group and the Saudi border. The Harrier would fly missions in between Maria's march zone and the Saudi border. The Harrier would also be used to assist Maria with anything that Maria thought useful.

Dan's second trip netted two Iraqi copters and approx 60 ground troops. Our second trip was uneventful, except for us dropping

Maria and her group. Maria found Iraqi ground troops withdrawing from the border, 16 tanks to be exact. Marina called in the Harrier and the Harrier made a total of six sorties, leaving all 16 tanks in smolders. Maria didn't take any prisoners, no she didn't kill them; she had them remove their weapons, pointed them north, and said to tell their brothers that she'd be there waiting.

Day after day it was much the same, each day, we saw less and less of Husain's military. For us things became routine. We didn't see any of the outside world, only the war. Evette worked hard and did a good job of keeping things going. On the third week, Evette said that the second New C-130 had been delivered to G.D. It would be ready for testing in a few days. I decided to bring that unit directly here to see what changes G.D. had made. As that C-130 arrived here, we would send Dan's C-130 back to Paxi. Dan, of course, would stay. We sent the Harrier back to accompany the Newest C-130 here.

On the way back to the states the Harrier suffered some kind of a major failure, and we lost it and the Pilot. An Israelis fuel tanker witnessed the explosion of the Harrier and said there were no verbal mentions of any problems, warnings, or ejection. The Israelis said there was also no debris or oil spot. As things went, our spare Pilot for the Harrier was sitting in our Saudi base. I was aware that Pearl and Rodgers were working with a new Harrier but, that I knew of it hadn't been tested. Without permission Pearl, flew the new Harrier to Fairbanks and would accompany the newest C-130 to our Saudi location. I had been warned that this new C-130 had not one but two of the Presidents men aboard.

While on its way to us while exiting Egypt's airspace, the C-130s TESS navigational Defense was activated. Pearl's Harrier's lock on was activated as it looked like the C-130 was about to fire on her Harrier. Pearl activated her stealth mode and took evasive movements but TESS did not fire its lasers. The Harrier's alarm was still activated, but still, the C-130's lasers did not fire. Whoever was in charge aboard the C-130 then had the Pilots change their destination. TESS then sent out a warning and self-destructed.

We didn't know how they had planned to avoid TESS's self destruct application, but whatever they planned didn't go as they had wanted. Pearl was attempting to communicate with the Pilots of the C-130 but got no reply. Pearl thinking of our people aboard and the need of the supplies that the C-130 was carrying was the only reason that she didn't down the C-130. Pearl didn't have to think about it long. As the C-130 started over the Red Sea, now heading south. Two fighter jets approached from the area of Yemen. Pearl saw their approach on radar; knowing the C-130 had that cannon on its port, she moved the Harrier to the starboard of the C-130. The lead jet coming in flew by the port of the C-130. Pearl's Harrier was again sounding the alarm of being targeted. Pearl's stealth mode still being activated, she then pulled the Harrier even closer to the C-130. As the second jet approached, it fired two rockets at our Harrier. Pearl then made a quick decision that could have cost her life. Pearl repositioned the Harrier just aft of the C-130 having the rockets slam into the C-130. As this happened, Pearl pulled up, missing the heat of the explosion of the C-130. As the first fighter jet came back around, the Harrier then again warned of more inbound rockets. Maybe Pearl's stealth kept her off the radar, but she was now being rocket chased from the heat that her Harrier was giving off. As she pulled up she deployed her heat flares. Pearl's flares worked, and she now knew she was in for a fight. We could now hear the conversation of all three jet pilots. Pearl was now talking to the two fighter Pilots. Not to our surprise, the two unknown fighter pilots were speaking English and sounded as if they were American. The C-130 that was fired on had gone down and crashed into the sea. Dan was in the air on patrol and, at the first sign of trouble, was heading to intercept the C-130, which was no longer the problem. Dan was in contact with the Saudi Air force and requested assistance of which he received at once. Pearl had engaged and fired a particular rocket she was given at Fairbanks. This rocket didn't seek out the tail flame but was guided by a satellite. Pearl's firing took out one jet, and then the second headed south. Pearl with her sassy voice called on the fighter that was fleeing to return and fight. Dan was up there now telling Pearl that she was not to follow. There was hesitation, but then Pearl heard my voice that said we had enough excitement for one day. Pearl said, Rodger that Commander and that she was on her way to the base.

Dan now still over 100 miles and closing, had captured the opposing Jets on satellite. TESS now gave us information that the single jet was an F15. Our satellite coverage now picked up that same F15 landing on a U.S. carrier. With our technology we would have the proof we needed that at least where the attack of our planes had come from. We figured that the mission of the two President's men aboard the C-130 had been to take control somehow and steal the plane with the newest TESS technology aboard.

Dan had now changed course and would return to base.

Pearl would soon be touching down at our Saudi Base. Once Pearl was down and safe, my thoughts went to our lost C-130 crew, then back to what Lori had said about me pulling Pearl into this mess. Pearl was now a seasoned fighter pilot, a pilot that had just shot down an F15 that belonged to not the Cubans, not the Russians but the U.S.

As Pearl landed, I was there standing on the runway. On Pearl's exit from the Harrier, Pearl referenced me as Commander, I her as Captain. There was a salute exchange then a long hug. I whispered in her ear that her mother was going to kill me. Pearl then said, you mean Divorce you. I then said yes, at least one of the two.

Pearl said she was pleased but didn't understand why TESS hadn't fired on her. Pearl noted that June had come to Paxi after the crash of the first Harrier and had brought with her the gold bracelet that Pearl had given to Sunshine. Pearl said that June had exchanged the one that Sunshine was wearing with the one that the Prince had given us. Pearl said that June said the bracelet would bring her good luck.

The Iraqis got pushed all the way back to Bagdad. Husain's army, as they retreated, set fire to every oil well in Kuwait they could; things looked a mess. We will be there until the end of March.

As we thought of rapping it up, I was summed to the Palace in Riyadh. Evette was upset, but I would leave her at the base. When I arrived, I was met by the Prince who accompanied me to the King. Before seeing the King, the Prince let me know how pleased the King was with our service. The King, the Prince said, wanted to keep our C-130s here on Saudi soil.

I explained to the Prince and the King that I could trust them, but, as they had witnessed, the U.S. President would stop at nothing to get his hands on TESS. The King said he understood my concerns but wanted a long-lasting relationship with such a group as ours. The King then handed me three envelopes. The King asked that I open the envelopes while in his presents.

The first envelope was what the King called his gift for our kind jester of assistance. For each of our personal that had lost their life in the line of duty, their families would receive $500,000. There was a check there for me for $200,000,000. There was also the title to the three C-130s that the King had purchased and sent to Fairbanks. There were two other checks, one covering the C-130 lost over the Red Sea and the other for the Harrier we lost. In all, the King was most generous.

The second envelope was a map and a handwritten statement from the King. The Prince made it clear the King's wish was I visit the ancient sight that they had found. Trust me, the Prince said, you will not be disappointed. The Prince reminded me that whatever riches found would be split down the middle, but whatever technology found would not be split but shared. The way the Prince spoke, as if they already knew what was down there. The Prince requested that while visiting the sight, our C-130s and Harrier be sent along. I looked at the map and said that the distance was too far from the nearest runway. The Prince said that during the last six months, they had built a runway large enough to land our C-130s and housing for a small group. Wow, a runway, I thought; this even more suspicion than they seemed to know what was down there.

The third envelope was a photo and the latest location of the Russian General. General Micoski, I said. The Prince then said ex-General. The King then noted that the General could wait as his men were at all times close by. The Russian was now in the northern part of Iraq fighting the Kurds.

I looked at the Prince and said that I would leave one C-130 here for the time being; the Harrier and the two laser batteries would be moved to Riyadh. Dan and Maria would stay. The Prince was happy and said he would see me again in 30 days at the ancient city.

June the children, and Sunshine were happy to see me. The big kids wanted to know about the war? Johnny had the most questions. I would only spend about a week at home. I would then travel to Miami to see Kay. I hadn't contacted Kay since our quite eventful one-night sailing trip. I was leaning against her mom's car in the Dade Junior College parking lot when she walked up to the vehicle. Wouldn't you know it, I'd been thinking about a girl for months that already had a boyfriend. The boy asked if I was her father? No I'm not kidding. Kay didn't act at all excited to see me. In front of the boy, Kay asked if I had just gotten out of jail? Kay turned and told the boy that she'd call him tonight, and with a peck of a kiss, he walked off. Kay then unlocked her car and got in the driver's seat. She grabbed the door, and I had to move back so she could shut it. She started the car while I stood there, then opened the window. What, she said, I don't hear from you for months, and you expect what? I don't even know you, she said. How about dinner, I asked? The window then went up, and the car started to back up. Then it stopped and started to roll forward. The car then stopped, and the window again went down. I suppose you know where I live, she asked? Yes, I answered. The Police came to my house she said, my mother is not going to be happy about me going out with you, my mother said I should stay as far from you as possible. The detective told us you were a dangerous person. She paused then said she didn't tell them anything. My mother doesn't know you were involved in the downing of the copters. 7:00 p.m. she said, bring flowers for my mom. I deserved what I got.

Kay's prettiness had all but gone. Besides, I didn't have an apartment or office in Maimi to wait at. I then thought I would try and find Rusty. I first stopped where he lived the last time I saw him.

Rusty hadn't lived there in years. I then went by his mom's; a neighbor said they had all moved to Georgia. Ralph too, I couldn't find, but Bernabe, now he was easy. His mom still lived down by my first elementary school.

Bernabe had gone off to a University in Mexico and become a Doctor. He now had an office at the Mercy Hospital Medical Center. Of course, he wasn't in the office; I left a message to call me when he got the chance. Within the hour, Bernabe called; he was busy with surgery all day but did give me Ralph's number. Bernabe laughed when he told me that Ralph was a well-known author and play write.

I called Ralph and we met down at the Sailing Club, no it wasn't my idea, Ralph was now a Sailing Club member and had his own sailboat. It was good to see Ralph; Ralph had been on two of my adventures, Zaire and Grenada. We talked about the old Boy Scout days, but mostly about Zaire or what he called the Angola trip. Ralph said the old Cuban that had gone with us had passed away two years back. Ralph said that he knew of, the old man took his part of the story to his grave.

While Ralph and I had went on to Zaire, we had left the old man at the airport on the Azores. The old man had sabotaged two Soviet air troop carriers by dumping molasses in their fuel. Both planes took off and had turned back with all four engines over heating; one made it back, the other did not. The old man had called the incident payback for the Bay of Pigs. We had traveled to Zaire to get Carson back; the Cubans had captured Carson and three others. That mission was a huge success, but Carson was never quite the same. Ralph and I could have talked for hours, but it was now past seven, and I still needed to buy flowers.

Arriving at Kay's House was like me going to pick up June the first time but worse. Kay's mom had me sit and wait while she put the flowers in water, then drilled me for at least 20 minutes. Kay's mother asked if I was married, how old I was, what I did for a living, and where I lived? When Kay walked out of her room, I stood and looked in amazement; I knew she was cute but didn't realize just how cute. She was beautiful. What came out of my mouth was, "I didn't know that Kay had a sister." It's me, silly, Kay said. Yes, mam, I see it now, I said. Kay had on a black dress that looked as if I could have found it in one of Lori's closets. How do you like it, Kay asked as she turned?

I didn't say what I was thinking; I just said she looked great. What wanted to come out of my mouth was that she looked good enough to eat.

Kay's mom said we should be back at a decent hour as Kay had school tomorrow morning. Yes, mama Kay answered back.

I was driving a rental, a small Mercedes. I opened the door for her; she stepped in. As I went to the first stop sign, she asked that we not go straight to diner but to walk on the beach. It was an easy choice for me; we went to that Key Biscayne lighthouse beach. We walked through the sand burs reaching the beach; Kay kicked off her shoes and walked into the small waves to get her feet wet. She turn and asked? What if I had gotten pregnant? Did you even think of that, she asked?

I did, she said; I worried about that, and those detectives who quickly found me. The detectives said that seven men had died that night and that they knew I was there when it happened. They said I was a suspect and that unless I talked about what happened, I might go to jail! There I was, having to deal with that and worry about being pregnant. You could have at least called, Kay said. I looked at her and asked if she would come out of the water and kiss me? Kay said she was thinking about it. She then took several steps and came into my arms. After that first kiss, she whispered in my ear that she was not pregnant. You do have an excuse for not seeing me until now, she asked? Yes, mam, I said, I was away at that Gulf War. Did we win, she asked? Yes, I said, I believe we did. You staying put for a while, she asked? I have a week before I need to return, I said. Kay then stepped back. A week then what she asked? Then I go back, I said. For how long this time she asked? A month or so, I said. Work or play, she asked? Work I said, the top-secret kind. You don't care that I have a boyfriend? I didn't know I said. You never asked, she said. If you don't have a girlfriend, why not take me with you, she asked? For one thing, you would be bored to death; the next thing, as you said, you don't know me. Do you plan on sleeping with me during the next week, she asked? I've been thinking about it, I said. Lots she asked? You ask a lot of questions, I said. She looked at me, well? I then kissed her again. You got a passport, I asked? Kay said she checked, and she didn't need a passport for Nassau. Nassau, no, but where you're going, you will.

Kay would be hungry tomorrow morning, as we didn't make it past the Sonora Hotel.

Kay still hadn't told her mom as yet; today, she was getting her passport. Kay would need a ticket with tomorrow's date on it, for the passport agency to issue a passport by tomorrow afternoon.

As things went, Kay's mother wasn't happy about her staying out all night or her missing school. When Kay informed her mom that she was going off with me, Kay's mom stopped her at the door. Kay's mom won the tug of war for Kay's suitcase. Kay walked out the door without it. Kay got in the car and said to drive. I looked at her and said to go back in. Kay looked at me and asked if I'd wait. Kay went back in, I waited. In twenty minutes, Kay reappeared with her suitcase. Kay's mom accompanied Kay to the car; I put Kay's suitcase in the trunk. Kay's mom asked to please return Kay unharmed. She's the only thing I have, Kay's mom said. Kay kissed her mom, and we were off.

I knew this wasn't exactly the way it should be, but having Kay along should make the time, especially the nights, go better. June wasn't going to be happy. It would only be a short matter of time before she heard. It wouldn't be today as Kay and I would fly directly to Paxi.

Kay's idea of Paxi before she saw it was Haiti. Haiti was known for Port-a-Prince and the country's overall poverty. Paxi was a part of Haiti, but for the most part, it was a fortress that included a small community of its own. It was a military compound that also housed the families of the men and women that served.

We took off from Miami in the Leer, and a short time later, we were landing at Paxi. Paxi was full of military, including two C-130s on the ground and one in the air. Pearl's three T28s were there, meaning that Kay would get to meet Pearl and maybe even Johnny. There was also one copter on the ground that Kay said was much bigger than the two that met their fate that night.

I warned Kay of Salinas's mother that was still there running the Chateau as she had for more than 30 years. We didn't have an old taxi pick us up; here; almost everything was military. In this case, a small troop carrier. I had told Kay that here at Paxi was her point of no return.

We were met at the chateau doors by Sharron; she was pleasant, asking only how her grandchildren were. I assured Sharron that Michelle, Kelly, and Jac were doing fine. There were at least 15 children there to meet Kay with Flowers. It seemed that Sharron had been passed the news that Lori was no longer the woman of the household. Once inside, one couldn't miss that portrait of Salinas. Kay stopped and looked up, saying how beautiful she was. I, too, looked up, thinking the same and also remembering how beautiful they all were.

I had almost had forgotten that Evette was here. Evette made her entrance from the pool side. Well, what do we have here? Evette asked, taking a look? Kay I said, this is Evette, Evette this is Kay. I see you didn't waste any time, Evette said. Evette then gave Kay a welcome aboard speech and said that the House didn't come with air conditioning, so a bathing suit was the dress of the day. Of course,

Evette had on nothing much of a bottom and a thin long sleeve top. Before we climbed the stairs, we both were served something cold to drink.

Upstairs were those four master bed rooms. Jack was here somewhere; Evette had one and looked like Sharron had the other. Our room, as did the others, had a complete balcony that faced out to the beach. As I stepped onto the balcony, I could imagine Salinas back then out there riding bareback on her favorite horse. Kay was changing and met me there, putting her arms around me and squeezing me in. It's beautiful here Kay said. I then shared what I had seen on my first trip here. Evette was here with us I said. Kay asked if Evette was ever my girl? I smiled and said no. I said that I had been fortunate, that I had been in love at least seven times. Two had left me. The other five had died. I turned and said that I hoped that fate had brought us together. Should I be worried Kay asked? I said that our first night could have gone the other way. Kay asked what was in the tubular box that I brought up on deck that night with the rifles? It was something that could have brought down one of the copters, I said, but only one.

Before dinner Kay met Pearl and Mr. Rodgers. Pearl, I told Kay, was up there that night.

Mr. Rodgers said that Pearl was a remarkable pilot along with being an aero engineer. Kay asked where Pearl had studied? Pearl said something about a school of hard knocks.

There were seven of us at the dinner table. We decided that we would leave tomorrow afternoon. The location of the Oasis was well into the interior of Saudi Arabia, far from any big or even mid-size cities. I didn't want Pearl to go but did want Mr. Rodgers along. I had this feeling in my stomach. Pearl said that if Rodgers and Kay were going, she would go. I expressed my thinking that sand could have had a bearing on the other Harrier crash. Mr. Rodgers agreed that the air filters could have been breached by sand passing into the engine. Mr. Rodgers noted that Pearl and himself redesigned the Harrier's air filters. The new filters would somewhat slow down the aircraft's speed and lower the power a bit, but the sand would not pose a problem.

Pearl, who had been in the desert, told Kay that the heat in the day and the cold of the night could be more than she'd be willing to bear. Pearl asked if Kay was ready to fight alongside us all? We, Pearl, said, are a family of peace-loving warriors. Kay looked at me and asked if I would stop Pearl's scare tactics. I looked at Kay and asked if they were working? Kay asked to be excused and left the table. Evette then said I should send Kay home. Pearl then got up and headed in the direction of where Kay headed as she had left the table.

When I arrived at my room, Kay was there already in bed. I went into the bathroom and called her in. Kay was slow getting there, but there she was. Now in the shower, I said that showers in the desert were not available every day. I held out my hand, and Kay took it.

Once in bed, Kay said that Pearl had come to apologize for the things she said. Kay said that Pearl said that I had many women but that her favorite was Lori. Pearl had told Kay that her mother left the Commander because I couldn't sit still. Not from the adventure nor sit still with just one woman. Pearl told Kay that if I chose her to become one of my companions, I would never leave her. Pearl said that either she would die with me, or she would one day leave out of jealousy. Whatever the case, Pearl told her, you will have to share him with his adventures and the other women. Kay said she asked Pearl if Lori would one day return? Just pray the Commander stays in good health, Pearl said.

Kay said she was scared, not of the heat nor the cold or the other women, but of me. Kay then asked what we were looking for.

I smiled and said that there were beings that came to earth many thousands of years ago. I believed they taught us their language and shared things that made for a better life here on earth. They were a people of peace but knew war only too well. We are looking for a lost city.

CHAPTER XIII

THE LOST CITY

WE ARE LOOKING FOR RICHES, Kay asked? No I said we are looking for technology. I then kissed her, and we were off to sleep.

We were all off as planned; Johnny had come over and said he was going along. It was Jack, Pearl, Johnny, 50 Black Devils, Evette, Kay and myself. We were all in for a real treat of a trip. A joke, of course, we were in the newest C-130; the noise and rough ride hadn't improved. Kay got airsick about 4 hours into the long flight. Our friends the Israelis were still doing the refueling. We would make a quick stop at Riyadh to pick up Maira and drop off Pearl to retrieve the Harrier.

Once again in the air, we were sent a coded GPS direction. Once we got close enough we were led in by Saudi fighter jets. We figured our destination would be about 1,000 miles into the desert. We hadn't ordered any equipment yet, but anything we needed would be flown in by one or both of Jerry's C-130s.

As we made our daytime approach, we saw no tower, only a newly paved runway. As we took a good look, there were dozens of workers clearing sand. The runway was marked by smoke at each corner. Jack and I were both in the cockpit; the Captain said it was putting a lot of trust in the Saudi's as we couldn't be sure the runway would hold up. The Prince had stated that the runway would hold. I could see no buildings nor an Oasis. The Captain put the C-130 on the runway without any problems. Pearl would come in behind us. Once our plane stopped, we got our first look at our transport. There being held by a group of Arab dressed men were several Camels, yes Camels and horses. Kay, who could barely stand, looked at the Camels, then at me, and said she was ready to return home.

The Prince himself was here mounted on his camel. The Prince assured me that we did not have far to travel. We were given some instructions and put aboard the animals. Kay was mounted with a rider that said Kay would be fine. Kay commented that it was easy for him to say.

We started up the first sand mound, when reaching the top of the mound, all the camels and horses stopped. The Prince didn't have to point it out; down below, there were Palms after Palms with what looked like a small clearing in the center. As we arrived, we could see a small tent city surrounding a small body of water. The place was beautiful; it had the appearance of a movie set. One of the Prince's men showed each group their tents. Kay and I were led to a beautiful large tent; inside we got a surprise, the King had Sent me a sort of gift. Standing there was a woman dressed in white linen, covering her from head to toe. The only visible part of her was the top of her nose to halfway to her forehead. The Prince had followed us in saying that this woman would be in charge of my care; she would feed me, bathe and comfort me. Kay then said, we'll see about that. The Prince just smiled and said the woman's name was Najima. Our belongings were brought into the tent, and then the Prince asked if I was ready to see what was so important? We walked out of the tent, and the Prince walked around the perimeter of the water, then stopped. Here the Prince said. Look into the water; when the sunlight is just right, you may see it. I looked and saw nothing; as I moved to my right, still looking into the water, I was startled! As I moved, it disappeared then came back to where I could see it again. It was all how the light hit the water. Below the water's surface I could see it! I almost couldn't believe my eyes. I then waded into the water to touch it. Below the surface only about two feet was what appeared to be a vehicle of some kind, with no appearance of a clear dome; it could be what I hoped was another vehicle. Maybe this was the third of what Victoria claimed was a total of four. I looked at the Prince and asked how long they had known? Come Commander the Prince said as he walked. As we walked past the palms, I could see two men were standing under what looked like a large makeshift lean-to. As we walked their way, the Prince waved his hand, and the two men pulled off a cover from something under the stand. The sand fell from the cover as it was being removed; again, I was Startled! Sticking out of the sand, I could see what looked like part of another vehicle; I then started almost running to see and touch what was there. As I arrived, I could see a vehicle partially sticking up from the ground and the rest hopefully buried in the sand. The Prince then asked if I was pleased? Come, he said as he walked back to the tents. As I looked back, the vehicle was now again covered. The two men stayed. By now Jack, Pearl, Johnny and Mr. Rodgers had caught up with us, them only seeing the part of the vehicle that was sticking up from the sand before being recovered. The Prince then stopped at another tent; the tent door was opened for him as he entered. Inside were blankets that had items laid out on them.

The Prince then said, once upon a time long ago, a people lived and thrived here. We believe that the water volume then was much greater and the Oasis much larger. We believe that there was a desert storm that buried most or all of the habitants. We gather that the ship while under the water can be self sufficient. We believe that the storm was so great that sands filled the water hole trapping the craft. Maybe they called for help, perhaps the help came, and they too were caught by the storm. Whatever happened, the Prince said, both ships were lost. The sand covered both ships for many years. A tribe of our nomads had for many years visited with and traded with the people of the Oasis, as they were called. The nomads had been visiting for years, but after the big storm, the Nomads could no longer find the Oasis. Years passed, and finally, the Nomads found Palms starting to grow and dug, finding water; the tribe began to revisit here once a year. Every time they came back, they found more items of gold and more water. Some years back, several items of gold started to appear on the black market where the Nomads traded. Soon the King sent someone to find this Oasis that bore items of gold. The King had some of the army stay at the Oasis looking for these items. Another storm soon produced the ship in the sand; a year later, the Kings-men spotted that ship in the water. And here we are the Prince said. What ever you need, he said you only need ask.

Jack and I made a list of what we would need; having already tasted the food, food was high on the list.

The day was not as hot as it should have been; my thought was the Oasis had something to do with it.

Pearl looked intrigued and anxious to get into these vehicles; it was her past and our future.

I was worried about Kay as her now being on the ground should have had her feeling better, but she was not.

Kay wasn't happy about sharing our tent with Najima, especially since Najima had made my bed not leaving a space for Kay, then making separate beds for Kay and herself. I said the day was not as hot as I thought it should be, but the night, even with Kay in my small bed, seemed particularly cold. During the night, Kay seemed to be getting sicker, running what I thought could be a fever. Najima said that Kay had a desert fever and should be sent back to the city.

The following day, I took Kay, one of the Prince's men, six of our Black Devils, and boarded our C-130 for Riyadh. With one more passenger, Najima. Najima said she would be punished if she didn't go with us. This didn't make Kay feel any better, but Kay was too weak to fight it.

Again the Prince's men cleaned off the runway from the accumulated sand.

Our C-130 crew had stayed with the plane keeping the motors and working parts from the sand. The Captain said he wasn't comfortable having the C-130 sit on the runway. When I saw the work involved and the possible consequences of some failure, we agreed that I would press for a hanger.

We landed at the Riyadh Royal Air Force Base. We were taken to a modern-looking Hospital. The Doctors did several tests on Kay and by late evening said that Kay had developed what they too called a desert fever. Desert fever they said, usually came when the body couldn't take the environment of the sand dust, the hot, dry air, and the cold nights. In other words, in a few days, Kay would be fine. Najima nor I left the hospital; I did get the chance to speak with Najima, mostly in Kay's private room while Kay slept. Najima said that she was a part of a nomad tribe that bandits had attacked; Najima said when the bandits attacked, her mother stuck a reed in her mouth and shallowly buried her in the sand. Once the bandits left, one of the badly wounded elders made it to her and pulled her from the sand. The old man, who was the only survivor besides me, died before anyone came by she said. I was only six years old and alone in the desert. The stars were in my favor, she said; a caravan of the King picked me up. They took care of me, and I was trained to be in the King's service. How did you learn my language, I asked? Najima thought about a second and said it must have been taught to her by her mother. A Nomad that spoke English, I said, must have been rare. Najima said that her mother spoke several languages and had many children, I was the youngest. All my family disappeared that day, she said. Najima said her Arabic name in English meant Star. My father called me Najima, but my mother called me Stella. Only my mother called me by that name. The caravan asked me my name, and I told them the name given to me by my father. What about you, Najima asked? The Prince said you go by several names. You are called Alshijae by the Arabs, Najima said. When the Prince talks about you when you are not present, he uses that name; when he speaks to you, he addresses you as Commander. Kay, Najima said calls you Jim. What name should I use when addressing you, Najima asked? Just Jim I answered. I will call you Alsadra, Najima said, yes she said, Nasir Alsahra. And what does that mean I asked? Najima replied Desert Eagle. I smiled and said I'd hold off on any nicknames.

After the third day, Kay felt better and well enough to travel. We, Kay and I would be heading back to Miami via Saudi Air. The C-130 would make daily passes along the Saudi Iraq border, then fly over the Oasis, then return to Riyadh. I would return to Riyadh from Miami. Najima said she would need to return to the Palace until I returned.

Kay and I were escorted by two of our Black Devils; Saudi Air flew into New York, there my men and I checked our arms at the check-in counter. We were told that the arms would be returned once landing in Miami. Kay slept most of the way to New York but from there we talked. Kay apologized for being what she called a disappointment. She said she knew that I would be well taken care of once I returned to Saudi Arabia. Kay was speaking of Najima. Kay laughed and said maybe Najima would be fat and ugly under all those clothes. Kay asked twice if she would see me again? I promised that she would.

We landed in Miami, and as we exited the plane, there was a welcoming party waiting. There were two detectives, at least eight Metro Police, and two or three from the FBI. We were all taken into custody, Kay going with two female officers, our two Black Devils going off with four police officers, and me going with the friendly Detectives, FBI, and two Metro Officers. The four of us were in handcuffs. I told Kay she didn't have to say a word.

I was being taken down town, me asking for my one phone call. I hadn't had an attorney in quite some time. Since the end of the Gulf War, Lourdes was back in Miami, and she was my call. I told Lourdes where I was and told her to get to Kay first. Lourdes knew what to do.

I, of course, was taken into one of those famous rooms where they would start playing good cop bad cop. I remembered Frick and Frack. It had been too long ago for any of these gents to have recalled.

For me, it was easy; I said I wanted to see my attorney.

It was a short wait; a group of three attorneys showed up, saying they would represent me. There were two men and a woman.

Two were brought in to see me while one went with the officers.

I was still in the cuffs and told the two with me that I could wait but that Kay was my primary concern. The woman said that another firm would represent Kay, and their responsibility was me. I looked at the woman and said that she better go and check on Kay, or they would all be fired. The woman then told her partner to go and check on Kay and report back.

The woman then said that I shouldn't be so concerned for the others as my charges could keep me locked up for some time. I asked what the charges were, and the woman said that as of the moment, the charges were pending. She continued saying that they claimed that I had shot down two unarmed helicopters in the bay, killing seven. She asked for my side of the story. I looked at her and asked if she had ever played Monopoly? The attorney then said this was serious. I said that Monopoly was a game of chance and that if she could check my passport, there inside tucked between the pages was a Monopoly card that was my get out of jail free. This is not a joking matter she said, if the girl was on your boat that night, she will, if she hasn't already give you up. I then asked about the cuffs? Do you think you could arrange to get these off I asked? The woman then stood and walked out.

By now the third attorney came back in with an officer that took off the cuffs. The woman attorney then entered and said that I needed to tell them what happen that night. I thanked them for getting the cuffs off and asked about Kay and my men? Kay is being held, the man said, and the two Haitians have been deported back to Haiti. Please the man said tell us about that night. As I told the detectives that morning. I did see two separate flashes that night; that's all I know. The man then said they had just been shown a video that showed what looks like you on your boat firing an automatic weapon at one of the copters. I have seen that video I said, and I can assure you it's a fake. The video I said is from a satellite that can be altered to show what they want. By now or within the hour, you will receive a similar video that shows two helicopters firing at the boat in the film and both copters being taken out by rockets that didn't come from any sailboat. Maybe they should be looking at where those rockets came from and why. As I finished, the other Attorney came back in and said they had been delivered a disk and that the FBI had also been delivered one.

A screen was then brought in, and the video played. The video showed what I said it did, it also showed that the rockets fired at the copters seemed to come from a fighter jet. When the tape finished, I said to tell the men from the FBI that if the girl wasn't sent home within 15 minutes, every news station in the country would receive our video plus the dossier of five of the dead men showing exactly what group they were employed by. I then looked at the Woman and said that maybe I wouldn't need that Monopoly card after all.

It wasn't another 30 minutes when I was returned my weapons and released. As we walked out to the street, where she was waiting, of course, it was Kay. Kay hugging me said she didn't tell them anything. I know I said, come let me give you a ride home. I turned and thanked the attorneys for their assistance, telling them to add Kay to their client list.

Lourdes was there with a car and my old friends, Big Ted and Steve.

As we stopped at Kay's house, their were two new cars in her driveway. I told her that all of her mom's debt had been paid and that a college fund had been set up for her. I offered Kay a job that would be there once she finished school. The summer I said could be spent working at the dig site or Paxi learning to fly. Kay kissed me, saying she knew she wouldn't see me again. I then mentioned that for the time being, there would be someone watching over her. She said she understood, kissed me then turned and walked toward the porch where her mother was waiting.

From there, I would be driven to Opa Locka airport, where Tommy was waiting. Lourdes said that June didn't know I was coming. I said it would be a good surprise for her and the children.

Arriving to Hill Top was a happy moment. June hugged me, not letting go, asking if I was by myself?

Somehow June had heard about the sailing club girl and mentioned that I always had a soft spot for girls at the club. June said something like that was alright as long as I didn't bring them home.

The children were amazing, how they had grown in such a short time. Sunshine was of course just as happy to have me home. Sunshine still wearing her back brace looked much better, with her Lilly white skin now having some color. June asked how long I was staying? I said I would be going back the next morning.

Dan had returned from the Saudi Iraq border with the number one bird; he said that a new C-130 was just days from being ready; it, the latest C-130, had been diverted to Paxi while still in the air heading to Fairbanks. G.D. had moved the TESS parts to Paxi in sections to discourage attempted theft. We were sure that the CIA remembered their last attempt to hijack TESS. The first time, back then, the CIA claimed that the attempt was made so by a group of rogue agents. The result, of course, was several dead and the Government declaring TESS a Top Secret Project. The second and most recent attempt during the Gulf War ended in losing one of their F15s, its pilot, two men from the CIA, one of our C-130s, and our crew.

Dan said that Cindy had called asking that he change places with Jack to get him home. I said that once Jack was away a month that we would send him home for as long as he could stay away. Dan had flown over with the same two members of the Black Devils that had been deported from Miami. I had given Dan instructions that he was to bring the newest bird to Saudi Arabia just as soon as ready.

The next day, after stopping at a Nassau bank, we then headed to Miami, making a short stopover, then myself and the Black Devils would be indirectly on our way back to Riyadh via Tommy's

Leer. On our way, we would first stop at Fairbanks, where I would exchange my briefcase with an identical one. The exchange at G.D. was made in John's office, him confirming that no one but him knew what I would be carrying. Our stop was short, from there only stopping for refueling. News of my return must have gotten here as Najima was at the Riyadh airport waiting. I carried only a brief case, my two sidearms, and a large suitcase. Najima was standing there, and when I walked up, she asked if I had brought her anything? Yes, I said, but you will have to wait for it.

This was as far as the Leer would go, Tommy with good reason, was worried about the sand getting into the engines.

We would be picked up and delivered by our C-130. Camels were waiting at the end of the runway. I had been gone just over a week, but the Oasis had changed quite a bit. First, there was the noise of the generators. Then, the Oasis pond was itself without much water. There were large plastic tanks everywhere that were either full of water or being filled. There was a large backhoe that had double-wide tracks. Over where the vehicle had been in the sand, there was now a larger tent. The vehicle in the water was now still there, but one part had been lifted, and men were digging mud and mining that mud through a sifter. There were tables that held what the mud had been holding. Jack saw us and came at a fast walk. Good to see you, Captain, he said. I hadn't seen Evette and asked for her? Jack smiled and pointed to one of the ones digging through the mud. Evette stood and called out for Najima to change her clothes and come and join them. Najima waved at Evette and yelled that she didn't have anything to change into. By now my briefcase and suitcase had been placed in my tent. I told Najima that I had picked up some clothes for her and that she could find clothes that should fit her in my suitcase. Are you sure Najima asked? Yes I said. Najima smiled and headed to the tent. Evette, now at my side, hugged me and asked about June and even Kay. The hug I received gave

Evette and Jack a laugh. It was so hot that the mud instantly stuck and caked on my arms and shirt. And Pearl and Rodgers, I asked? Jack pointed to the tent that covered the one vehicle. Jack said that Rodgers couldn't stop touching it. Jack asked if I had brought the Keys; I nodded that I did. I then walked toward my tent; I was going for the key cards when I opened the tent, where she was staring at the clothes I had purchased. Well, I asked what's the story? Do you like what I picked out for you? Najima then said that she had never worn a pair of pants before. Ok I said, you take that off and I'll assist in putting the new clothes on. Najima then pointed me to the doorway. I grabbed my briefcase and said I'd be with Rodgers trying to open the door. What door she asked? The vehicle door, I said. Hurry, or you'll miss it.

When I reached Rodgers, there he was scrapping and cleaning looking for a door way. The vehicle was sitting on the hot sand under the shade of the tent. Still, the vehicle was hot to the touch. I was worried that this key might not be the same, and even if it was, there might not be enough stored power to open the door. I was ready but was waiting for Najima to get there. Looking in the direction of my tent, here she game. Boots, jeans, long sleeve shirt and a shaded hat. It was the first time I saw her entire face. When she got under the shade, Evette was the first to comment. Well, little sister, you don't look half bad. I turned and looked at Pearl, you ready I asked? I placed in one of the two cards. Nothing, then something, then nothing, then, the door popped open. The door was now opened about 2 inches. When it opened, the smell that came out was that of death. I then placed the chain with the two key cards securely around my neck. With heavy gloves on, Jack, Rodgers, and I grabbed the door and began to lift it. The door moved up, but not even a light came on. This looked like the exact vehicle we had taken from the TOTO channel. I folded down the steps and started in.

With a flashlight in hand, I confirmed that this vehicle was identical to the first one. I explained to Rodgers about the Power rods, and maybe, just maybe, there might be enough power to start the electric water pump. We would first need water and lots of it. We had the backhoe move water while Jack got what hoses we had. Rodgers and I suited up and would be checking the power rods.

We were in luck after so many years; both spare rods seemed to show some power. It would take us over two hours to change the rods, the stench that didn't leave made me believe that once we got lights, we would likely find several skeletons.

Rodgers and I overlooked the time, it was late, but I didn't want to leave the vehicle's door open, leaving the controller open to theft. It's was 4:00 a.m. when we attempted to turn on the power on. The control panel lit up; we were running bare minimum with power only showing at 15%. The water was hooked up, and I turned on the water pump. We stayed until we saw that the pump was doing what we hoped it would, raising the power level by one percent. We didn't look though the vehicle, we would leave that until later in the morning after some food and rest. In my case, rest. When we exited the vehicle, I pushed in the key card, and the vehicle's door shut tight. Jack was the only one still there; we talked a moment about the security then I was off to my tent. There was a small lamp on, I noticed that my bed was larger than before, and Najima's bed had been moved much closer to mine. Najima's covers were pulled over her head, me just then noticing the cold. I was pooped, I dropped my clothes and was in my bed. I think I was asleep before my head hit the cushion. I usually only sleep on each shoulder for an hour before I needed to roll over. Those old shoulder injuries of the past. As I rolled over, I felt the comfort of something that felt like silk with all the curves. The smooth curves didn't move; I put my arm around her and fell back to sleep.

The darkness of the tent wouldn't let you know if it was daylight. I looked at my watch and saw it should now be morning. I didn't need to see to know that Najima had gone from my bed. I then saw some sunlight when the tent door was pulled back, me seeing Najima coming in with food. At this point I wasn't that hungry. I sat up and called her to my bed. Najima was again wearing her original robe, I threw my cover back and held out my arms. The food will get cold, she said.

When Najima redressed, it was now the shirt and jeans. We had eaten and had what they called tea.

Once at the Vehicle, I put in the key and the door opened upward on its own power. Inside I found the lights; the power was now at 25%. With the lights now on, Najima and I saw eight skeletons, all looking to be women and children. The bones looked wrapped into one another as if they were hugging together when they died. The Prince's theory seemed to be very close to what might have happened. It looked as if each remains were wearing that same gold bracelet that the King had sent as a gift. When Najima saw the bracelets, she looked shocked; she then looked at me and pulled up her long-sleeved shirt; there, tightly on her wrist, was a matching gold bracelet. Najima was speechless; I stood and rolled her sleeve down, covering what I had seen. I couldn't help but smile with some pride. I then hugged her, saying that maybe these were her people. I then looked into her light green eyes seeing tears rolling down her cheeks. The Prince, I said, he must have suspected. I was as gentle with the bones as possible. I did not remove any of the bracelets nor any other jewelry items. I did see and remove one set of card keys that were around one skeleton's neck. Najima looked at me and said it was alright. We would box up the bones and remove them from the vehicle. Jack was now inside with Rodgers, trying to get seated in one of the small control seats. Jack was with Rodgers telling him not to touch anything. Power was still slowly raising. It was time to try the atmosphere control as the heat was becoming unbearable.

Pearl was at the door and wanted in, but the space wouldn't allow it. I asked Rodgers to exit the vehicle; he was hesitant but did as I requested. Pearl then came in for the first time; Pearl said it somehow looked familiar. Do you think you could fly her, I asked? Pearl said that the area where we were was a good practice ground. I told her that the power required for the lift would need to be close to 100%. That I said would take another two days or so. I asked that she and Johnny sit at the controls and learn what each switch was. I warned to stay clear of the weapon systems. I then went down the small steps to unlock the weapons cabinet; the original vehicle had two laser weapons. Here the two lasers were there and fully charged. We hailed Maria who was with her men digging. I removed one of the lasers and handed it through the opened door to Maria. I asked her to check it, and if it worked, she was to keep it close by at all times, her guarding the vehicle and five men guarding her. I then took a ride to the C-130 to use the computer. I would ask Jerry to send one of his C-130s to retrieve the two laser cannons at our original Saudi base. Najima, who had gone to the plane with me, asked if I would report to the Prince of our progress? I told her that TESS had picked up transmissions from the Oasis camp. The new TESS could pick up a message in Arabic and translate it into another, in this case, English. I did not indicate it was her, but Najima took it as such. I am loyal to my King, she said, but I have chosen you for my husband. My husband will always come first, she said. I will keep my agreement with the King and the Prince, I said. I am worried that with power comes the greed of such. Here we hold an earthly power of greatness that can do good or evil. What will you do with your power, my husband, she asked? At present it keeps me from being a better father and maybe husband. The protection of my family comes first. Kay, I said will not be my wife, I did not pick her for such. I looked at her and said that I looked forward all day to holding her again tonight. Najima smiled, I pulled her to me and kissed her. Najima was shy with her kisses, which I was sure would change. On the Camel ride back to the camp, we talked of what she remembered as a child. Najima said that other children made fun of her because she was different. She said that the King had many wives and many sons. One of the sons had died, and I was brought to the mother of the boy that had died. She was a good woman who treated me well. Shara had another son my age, and we grew up together. Harag and I were separated at age 12, but he stayed in contact with me until he went into the military. The Prince is Harag's older brother. The Prince changed how I was treated at school. Harag got into a fight with another of the King's son's children because I was not of royal blood. Harag was winning the fight when others jumped in, I to jumped in. Harag's brother the Prince, then entered the fight. The Prince whipped them all, she said. The Prince announced that he would beat anyone who mistreated me. A good big brother I said, yes Najima said, the best. I then turned my Camel around, heading back to the C-130. Najima asked why I was returning? I said I had one more message to send. Najima waited with the Camels while I reinterred the plane's cockpit. I sent one more message, and we were on our way. Najima didn't ask, but I believed she knew that my message was to the Prince.

At the camp, we were almost ready to open the second vehicle. The vehicle that had been in the sand had its inner door open. We couldn't be sure that the vehicle sitting in muddy water didn't also have its inter door open. If its inner door was open, and we opened the outside door, then when we opened the outer door, the water could rush into the main cabin then down into the lower level, which held the engine and power source. That, I thought, would not be good.

Once we freed the vehicle from the mud's hold, we removed a small portion of the tent placed over our work area, then used the backhoe and raised the section that housed the Vehicle's door. The tent's cover was then placed where it had been covering our workers from the sun but most importantly hiding what we had found from any passing satellites. The opening of the vehicle's door would be much like the other. Again with the smell of any remains. This time the cabin had many more bodies. Still using portable lighting, we counted the bodies by the number of bracelets. By the numbers, it was evident that they had suffocated in what they believed was their last chance of survival. We would work through the night removing the bones, again placing the bones in boxes without removing any bracelets or jewelry. These bodies did not produce any more key cards. Again we couldn't take the chance of leaving the door open nor closing it then not being able to reopen it.

The bodies were removed and I got down below, here the spare power rods were at zero charge. Our only option would be to wait until the first vehicle's power rods were charged and bring one rod to install here in the second vehicle. I decided to remove the controller and take it to the first Vehicle for safekeeping. Once in the first Vehicle I removed the second laser gun and placed it with the second vehicle's guard group. This time Najima had worked with me until we couldn't do any more. We were all quite tired; Najima and I would go directly to our tent. Najima turned the small lamp down to where there was little light, I turned it back up. Najima said she had never undressed in the presents of a man before. I then said that I wanted to see her Beautiful skin. It was true that Najima had a head full of hair, but it was also true that she only had four toes on each foot. I mentioned that almost all of the skeletons we saw today only had four toes. Najima reminded me of the fight that broke out at her school. We all wore sandals, she said; they teased me because my feet were not like theirs. With the light now lowered, I opened my briefcase, bringing out a piece of jewelry that had come from the Shah's Treasure. Although I had not seen all the jewelry that we had brought up from the sea, I remembered this one piece. It was modest in size compared to some of the other jewelry, but its beauty had caught my eyes. I took the neckless and Najima now on her knees; I put the neckless around Najima's neck and locked it in. Najima, without even getting a good look at it, said it was beautiful. She then turned and turned the lamp almost entirely down.

The few hours of sleep we needed would not be. We were alerted that there were several fighters approaching, with a larger plane also on its way. Jack nor myself would be able to reach the C-130 before it lifted off. I ordered the guard to get Evette and Rodgers and meet me at the first Vehicle. Once at the first Vehicle, I found that Pearl and Johnny were inside with the door shut. I placed in the card key, and the door opened; I ordered Evette, Rodgers, and Najima inside and would shut the door behind me. I then ordered the second door of the second vehicle also shut, this knowing the risk of it not opening again.

Our ground personal had taken cover, Jack now holding one laser gun and Maria manning the other. We did not know for sure whom was on the way, but as the first fighters zoomed by, the roar that followed had Jack say that they were F14s. We noted that several of the neighboring countries have these jets, including the Saudi's. Three jets flew over without firing. The radios that Jack and I had in hand, started jabbering. The unknown jets hadn't caught our C-130 off guard as they planned; our grounded C-130 had activated their systems and navigation block. The incoming larger plane was still heading our way, they may turn off, but they could, by chance, fly over. Them planning on landing wasn't a possibility; we figured that their plan must have been dropping Paratroopers. The

Crew of our C-130 said that the Jets had wanted to drop some kind of weapon on the camp or at least the runway, but their electrical had been jammed, not permitting whatever action they had planned. The C-130 crew continued on reporting that once the jets got out of the maze, their loads had dropped somewhere out in the desert. Their loads dropping meant that they had planned an attack. We then heard our C-130 captain warning off the larger plane that was still heading our way. Our Captain stated that they were considered hostels and would be brought down by laser fire. Into our Captains second verbal warning, the large plane turned and headed toward the Red Sea. We then heard a familiar voice, it was Dan calling from the third new C-130. Dan said that the F14 bandits and the larger cargo plane had originated from Libya. Good to hear your voice I said. I asked if they could stay up there until Jack could be dropped off in Riyadh?

The excitement was over for now. The Prince would be arriving sometime about mid-day.

Najima and I would get back to sleep. Daybreak came, and the door of the second vehicle did not pop open. I hoped that with the heat in the vehicle rising by the minute that the pressure could help with the door. Sure enough, the hot sun did the trick, my key card had unlocked the door, and the sun's heat supplied the pressure to open the door by itself.

When the Prince showed, we now were running a 24 hour skywatch.

The Prince was fascinated by the two vehicles and our ongoing work. We were presently in the process of moving one of the 75% charged power tubes from the first vehicle to the second. Once switching the tubes and returning the second vehicle's controller, we had the two vehicles each showing about 35% of their power. Now the priority was getting the water hooked up to the second vehicle and getting the water pump to start pumping and producing electricity. We calculated that it would take three or four days to get the power rods to 100%. With the water pumps working and producing the current to recharge the connected power rods, the second vehicle's door was shut with no one inside.

The Prince asked what would be the next step and how long before bringing in a few pilots? I gave the Prince something to think about. These ships were not built to crash, there are no seat belts. Here any crash would most likely kill the occupants and damage the Vehicle, possibly beyond repairs. We didn't have spares and couldn't as yet match the materials.

I did, however, deliver the Prince something he could take back to the King. I gave the Prince one of the two laser guns from the first Vehicle. I warned of its capabilities and that its security was of the utmost importance.

Najima was now at my side most of the time; the Prince almost ignored her; I asked why and the Prince said it was because of her dress. Although Najima had her blouse buttoned up to the top, the Prince had noticed the neckless and said that an Arab woman could only receive such a gift from her husband and, by wearing such, was announcing to the world that she was married. Looking at me then at her, the Prince said that divorce was not an option and that a woman separated from her husband would become an outcast. Looking at Najima, the Prince said clearly that she was only to address himself or other Royalty when she wore the clothing of a married Arab woman. He looked at me and congratulated me on picking such a wife, then wished me many children and much happiness. The Prince then smiled and noted that the King would approve.

The Prince was aware of the attack from Libya and said that they would send notice to that leader of the King's displeasure. Libya had been quiet over the past four years; that was when the U.S. Bombing took place in retaliation for the bombing in Berlin was linked to the

Libyan regime. The Prince would not stay overnight; he left saying that he'd return after the full moon passed.

Jack had been dropped off at Riyadh and was now on his way home to Cindy. I had been worried about the home front and Paxi.

Pearl was again sitting with Rodgers at the first Vehicle's controls studying how things worked. I had mentioned Maximus's name to Pearl, but she asked me to hold off. He has to know what's going on, Pearl said.

Jerry was to bring both ground lasers to the Oasis, but the King had requested that both units be brought to Riyadh to be permanently installed at the palace. We would do as the King requested as G.D. had now readied two more ground lasers. The lasers from the Saudi Iraq border would be moved to Riyadh while the two new units were moved to the Oasis.

That night in our tent, Najima said she was mostly pleased with what the Prince had said about our marriage and asked if she should worry about becoming an outcast? I, am not an Arab, I said, but if I were, I would consider you for one of my wives. I thought that would upset her, but Najima seemed happy with my reply.

The next several days were spent checking with Pearl's progress and digging for other items that should show something about how these beings had survived out in the desert. We had now placed the second vehicle on padding high enough that we could return most of the water into the ground of the Oasis. The water level was much lower than it had been. The digging brought out lots of items, and we had so far located another 16 bodies. Strangely enough some of the bodies found did not have the Golden bracelet, and those without bracelets had five toes on each foot. This to us meant that at least when the sand storm hit there had been others at the Oasis. Maybe they were living there, and perhaps they could have been trading and or there seeking refuge from the storm. The bodies of the five-toed bones all had some form of jewelry. One body's jewelry was filled with what looked to be Chinese markings and inscriptions to include a ring that could have been used as a seal and a large engraved bracelet. Since I believed that these two items were significant. I removed them to see what we could learn of whom this visitor could have been and why he was there.

We found bones of Camels, goats, sheep and even dogs. On the third day of digging we found a being with our same key cards and a strange medallion around its neck. This being also had a belt with a laser hand weapon with other small looking devices including what looked to be a earthly made knife. This being also had the bracelet and a ring. Close by we found what I believed must have been the being's dog. Along with this dog's bones contained what I though was a not so common dog collar. The collar was flexible and made of that same gold material as the beings bracelets. I would also personally removed the items from that special being's skeleton along with his dog's strange collar. I checked, the dog had 5 toes. I placed the ring and bracelet on the chain with the medallion that I took from that same skeleton. Then placed the chain around my neck. I cleaned up the belt and the items it had held. Once cleaned I then wore that same holster, it now holding the small laser, knife, and dog collar.

Pearl, Johnny and Najima helped me bury the dead that we had wrapped in material found within the Vehicles. It was Pearl's idea to place in the grave a GPS locator that maybe one day someone could retrieve the bones for a better ceremony.

On the fourth day of the restart of charging, both vehicle's power rods were showing at 100%. We would then exchange one power rod that was 100% with one of the spares. Now both Vehicles's power were at 50%. We would do this twice to have the Vehicles and spares at 100%.

CHAPTER XIV

OUR FIRST LIFT OFF

ONE WEEK LATER, EVERYTHING WAS at 100%, and Pearl was ready for a trail lift-off. The Prince returned and was there when Pearl and Johnny, at the controls, lifted from the sand. We were ready for the sand, and it was a good thing as the sand was so thick that when we could see again, the Vehicle was gone. Looking up into the sun we couldn't find them, but they were there hovering. Pearl brought the vehicle back down with the same amount of blown sand coming our way. Once down the door opened and out came Johnny first then Pearl. When Pearl walked through the vehicle's door, Pearl had her flyers hat in her hand. This was the second time Pearl showed her bald head in public, the first when meeting Sunshine at the airport in Nassau.

Maybe Rodgers had known, but the others except Johnny had no idea. All including the Prince had noticed that the skeletons with their special bracelets had larger than normal heads. With Pearls flyers hat off, that big head of hers stuck out like a sore thumb.

Pearl came to me and hugged me saying that she always knew she was born to fly as a free bird. Pearl then looked at the Prince and asked if he'd like to take a ride. The Prince looked at me, then

Najima, take Najima the Prince said, take Najima. Najima looked at me for approval; I nodded my head yes. I pressed the button on my radio and told Dan that Pearl was going for a ride and to be on his toes. Dan said that they were up there and ready.

For the first time, we had both of our Newest C-130 in the air; one had Maria aboard and was circling at about 50 miles, the other with Dan being much closer. With Najima aboard, the vehicle door was closed and we were on the ground again receiving that sandblast.

As yet, we on the ground didn't have contact with the vehicle. The vehicle contacted TESS on Dan's C-130, and Dan could relay what was said to me via radio.

Dan and I knew this would be seen by several satellites as after the incident with Libya, several satellites had been repositioned to cover our position. The Prince had been made aware of this before our test flight and agreed to go ahead.

Looking up into the sun light, the sun was all we could see. The Vehicle had gone. For some reason I wasn't worried a bit. Dan's voice came on saying that Pearl had asked to let TESS use it's navigational block to see what effect it had on the Vehicle. I approved but warned to proceed with caution.

TESS's navigational block could now include messing with Satellites. The C-130 that Dan was in had the controller that we retrieved from the facility that Pearl's grandfather had built in the cave that ran under the Naval base on Andros. We had good reason to believe that the facility had been built as a hideout from another group of beings that had been searching to destroy them.

Dan now alerted that Israelis and the U.S. had directly dispatched fighter jets to investigate the interference to their satellites. ETA on the Jets would be within 15 minutes. The Saudi military command had now warned off the Israelis. The U.S. military was asked to hold their jets back. Our second airborne C-130 had also activated its TESS, making the Navigational situation reach an additional 100 miles out. Dan now said that Pearl had breached the guarded perimeter and was directed to return to base. Pearl, being Pearl, did not immediately respond to Dan's order. Our second C-130's captain noted that Pearl had now left even his perimeter. That same captain then said that Pearl had now exited Saudi air space. Dan then said that he now had confirmation of Pearl's return. Dan said that it looked like both the U.S. and all except one Israeli jet had turned back. The one that did not was now heading directly toward the camp. The Israeli jet could not count on it's navigation and would pass though our circle without being able to take photos; however, the F15 had visually spotted Pearl and had changed direction to get a better look. Pearl also spotted the fighter and decided to give the fighter something to talk about. Pearl came within feet of the fighter. By the time the fighter came back around, Pearl was gone. The fighter now being disoriented, came out from our navigational block and was heading directly toward Riyadh. Riyadh had dispatched a group of F14s that surprised the Israeli fighter; two of the F14s quickly fired on the F15, hitting it, causing the pilot to eject.

The Saudi fighters excitedly reported that they had shot down an Israeli F15 that was headed toward Riyadh. Saudi helicopters were on the way to recover the Israeli pilot.

Pearl's landing was the same with the sand. When the vehicle door opened, it was Najima that first exited with her arms halfway up, palms up in the air. Her first words were praise to Allah. It then was Pearl's turn to exit. Pearl almost pushed Najima aside to get to me. I was expecting a hug, but it wasn't to be. The pilot she asked?, then looking at the Prince she said, please do not harm him; he meant you no harm. The Prince then turned and spoke in

Arabic to one of his men. The Man whom the Prince had spoken to then ran and jumped on a horse and headed to their small jet. Our orders on such should be to take prisoners, the Prince said. Pearl then looked at me and asked if she could go to him; Najima said she would change clothes and accompany her. Najima then looked at me for my approval. As Najima hurried away, the Prince yelled to remember that she was Arab and a married woman. Dan was landing on the runway, I radioed, saying he would deliver Pearl and Najima to Riyadh Royal Air Base. The Prince then said that his king would be pleased by today's events. While Dan waited on the runway, he mentioned that the Americans were not happy and that the Israeli radios had gone silent. Also silent were the Saudi radios on the Israeli pilot.

The Prince said his goodbyes and now asked if we could move one or both of the Vehicles to his Riyadh base? I was blunt, if he wanted, I would deliver the first Vehicle upon Pearl's return, but the other I would keep with me. The Prince said the King may disapprove. I looked at him and said that the treasure here were the Vehicle's, and the agreement was that we would divide what we found, 50, 50, and share all technology. The Prince looked at me and said he would consult with the King.

As the Prince was leaving, I asked Rodgers if he thought anyone else could fly that thing? Rodgers reply was, only Maximus. Rodgers said that the radar was unlike anything he had ever seen; it was like sitting within a holly gram with everything moving all at once but without really seeing it. And yet Rodgers said, Pearl sat there playing with it as if it were a toy.

Dan said that they were now in the air and there was an urgent call from the Admiral to contact him at once. I asked Dan to get back to Lourdes to contact the Admiral and tell him that I was out fishing without radio contact. If it was genuinely urgent for him to tell Lourdes or contact Jack, who was at Paxi.

The message back from the Admiral was that I should come to visit within the next 24 hours, or my midair refueling would be cut off. This threat wasn't so significant at the moment. Presently where we were good with the fuel.

My main in air refueling was the Israelis, who probably weren't too happy with me. For the Israelis the Saudis were by far the most friendly of all the neighborhood. Up until and including today the atmosphere between the two had been confrontational.

With today's actions and the Prince's new request of moving both Vehicles to Riyadh, my planning would need fuel if we all were to make it home. Paxi now had it's own sea buoy for ships and a pipeline to receive fuel from any size tanker. Such fuel was stored in underground fuel tanks. Home, thinking of Nassau and Paxi, were close enough to our ground fuel supply to continue doing what we did in that air zone, without in air fueling. Here we were thousands of miles from home with two C-130s and Pearl's Harrier. It was getting late, and I began to worry about Pearl and Najima.

The next morning we received good news, the Israeli pilot had been sent home, and the girls were on their way back. Once Dan was close enough to cover us at the camp, I had the other C-130 land so I could communicate with Lourdes using our computer code. I finished and the C-130 went back up. Dan landed, and the girls came walking down the ramp, then Najima started to run. When Najima, still in her Arab dress, hit me with her hug, it almost took us both down. Najima looked at me and said that she had missed me terribly but was not sorry that she had gone with Pearl. Pearl now getting to us, said that we now had one more friend. I looked at her and said the pilot. Pearl said yes then said he was very handsome and had promised to visit her in Nassau. Pearl laughed when she said the the young pilot said he would teach her some flying tricks. Pearl said that they hadn't told the flyboy that it was them in what the Israeli pilot had called a spaceship. Pearl said that Najima was a big help in freeing the pilot. Dan walked down the ramp and said there was lots of chatter going on that I should hear. Dan pointed me up to the cock pit. Once up there, TESS had picked up transmissions in Arabic as TESS translated. Seemed that there would be a large air and ground movement planned for our area. I didn't like it. I was in the cockpit alone for quite some time.

It was going to be difficult for me to tell Najima my plan; I quietly asked Pearl, Johnny, and Rodger for another test flight this afternoon. We would be testing the second Vehicle. If good to go, we would soon be pulling out. I contacted the Prince and told him that we would move the first tested Vehicle tonight to Riyadh, using the dark as cover.

Once I had Najima alone, I asked her to make a choice that I didn't think was fair to ask, but under the circumstances, I needed to. I told her that we would be soon leaving the camp and would let the Prince's men complete the dig site. Najima said that she knew where the radio that the Prince's men were using was located. Najima said she would show me when I was ready. Najima said that she would always consider this her place of birth but that she had chosen me as her future and was 100 % mine. Najima also said that Pearl had told her of her family's extraordinary adventure to come to this planet and the sacrifices her people had made for thousands of years. Najima said that Pearl said that the threat was still out there and could at any time return and make war on them and all humans.

The testing of the second vehicle went well. While Pearl and Johnny were testing, myself and Rodgers were busy making a small but significant change in the first Vehicle.

Pearl and Najima would again ride with the wind in the first Vehicle. The vehicle was delivered to Riyadh without problems. The delivered vehicle was moved into a large Concret hanger. The Prince was there to receive the vehicle personally.

Pearl and Najima were then picked up by Dan's C-130 and returned to the Oasis camp. A surprise was waiting Pearl, the Israeli pilot that she had met in Riyadh had dropped in via parachute. I had requested this pilot from the Israelis. If we were to leave tonight, we needed a pilot to fly out the Harrier. Rubin, the downed Israeli pilot, had, of course, volunteered. Rubin would pilot out the Harrier.

Najima pointed out the radio, the Prince's men were disarmed and the radio confiscated.

We would take our equipment, the second vehicle, both sets of key cards, the medallion that was found with the second set of key cards, the gold wrist bracelet, the waistband with the hand laser, the ring, the three lasers weapons from inside the vehicles, the dog collar, and what I believed to be a ring and bracelet showing some form of a Chinese connection, our share of the items found, plus of course, Najima.

Pearl and Rodgers would fly the vehicle, the Israeli pilot the Harrier, Dan, Johnny, and Evette in the one C-130 and myself, Najima and Maria in the other. In a matter of hours, we were all in the air and out of Saudi air space.

Earlier that morning, I had requested two things from the Israelis, a pilot for the Harrier and the refueling. No one would have wanted the Saudis to have both vehicles, even if they didn't have a pilot. The Saudis now had in their hands the technology to develop what I had over the past years. This if they didn't lose it by theft or accidentally destroy it first.

CHAPTER XV

GENERAL SANTOS

WE WOULD ALL ARRIVE AT Paxi without any interference. The Israeli pilot would always be loyal to Israel; Pearl asked that we keep him. Pearl was, of course, a one of a kind woman, but she was a woman. Rubin said that he had some leave time coming and, if permitted, would like to return to visit. Pearl, of course, liked that idea. I reminded Pearl of life's choices. I told her that time was on her side as she was still young, but that there was still much to do.

Pearl looked at me and asked if it was fair to say that I somehow got to have my cake and eat it too? Pearl then asked, speaking of too much cake, what are you going to do with my sister? Pearl was of course, referring to Najima. And don't forget my mother, Pearl said. My kind, Pearl said, picked only one wife; it appears you have three. My reply was that in my world, I didn't have a wife. I have one ex-wife and two lovers. Pearl smiled and said she couldn't wait to see how long that lasted when June met Najima. The cat and the mouse Pearl said. Only the cat stayed at home while the mouse went off to play. The mouse is coming home with something that will make the cat very angry.

Pearl would show Rubin the Paxi facility and the Chateau. Of course, they would all meet Salinas's mother, Sharron, and see that grand portrait of Salinas. It was Najima that starred so at it. She was beautiful Najima said. Yes, I said, it was her choices that killed her.

Of course, we had received several messages while on the flight home, the Prince, the Admiral, the Director, the Israelis, and the Iron Woman. I responded to all that I was on vacation with my family and would be in touch when I returned. My added message to the Prince was that I had lived up to my agreement, and they owed me nothing. I said that the card key to their vehicle would be delivered once I safely returned from my vacation. I thanked him and the King for their kind hospitality but said that I was worried that moving both Vehicles to Riyadh could have brought us to conflicting interests. I noted that if they used their new power well, they should not require any further assistance. However, I would keep the channels of communication open.

My fondest reply was to the Iron Lady, adding that I had not forgotten her most generous assistance in my time of need. I would visit her at the end of the Summer.

Najima and I would not spend the night, I wanted to get home and see the children and June. For me, it was time for that shot of medicine. When we boys were sick, my mother would give us a tablespoon of castor oil. It was terrible stuff but bearable. I once saw my brother tell my mother his sore throat was too painful to swallow the castor oil. My father then took an empty ice cream stick and wrapped it with toilet paper, poured mercurochrome on the paper, and swabbed it down my brother's throat. After witnessing that, I never have complained of a sore throat since.

I hadn't seen June in months, and now coming home, I would be bringing home another remarkable woman.

When we drove up to the Hill Top house, it's was just about dark. We hadn't surprised them as Lourdes had kept June abreast of our every move. June knew that we had lost a set of crew members along with one of our new C-130s.

The children all came running to see Papa; June walked out looking like a million. June walked right by Najima and kissed me, not letting go. June then turned and looked at Najima; June clearly said that she was welcome here but would not be sharing her bed with another woman. June then looked at me and said I had been away from her too long. By now, Najima had also been attacked by the children, a different type of attack. June took my hand, and the children took Najima's. I looked around and did not see Sunshine; where is she? I asked loudly? June asked who? Then Sunshine jumped up from behind the couch, Me she said! Sunshine! I then dropped June's hand, meeting Sunshine halfway. Sunshine's hug had tears involved, both ways. She said she had removed her back brace only so that she could hug me. From my hug, I turned and pointed Sunshine to Najima; look, I said I brought you a new friend. Sunshine looked at Najima from head to toe, walked to her, and lifted her left sleeve. Somehow Sunshine knew that the bracelet would be there. When Sunshine confirmed the bracelet, she let out a cry of joy! From the cry, Sunshine then turned and came to me again with another hug. Then Sunshine turned and went for Najima. Now Sunshine was hugging Najima. Still hugging Najima, Sunshine said, my name is Sunshine; what is yours? Najima said Najima. Najima, of course, had to see Sunshine's bracelet and recognized the oversized head. The children didn't quite understand what had just happened but June surely did. I went to my briefcase and opened it, avoiding the rat trap. I then pulled out the gold bracelet and placed it on June's left wrist. The ring was now on my finger, the bracelet was now on June's left wrist, and the Medallion, well, it along with the other items would, for now, be put into safekeeping.

The happiest of everyone was Sunshine. Sunshine hadn't as yet let go of Najima's hand.

Betty was watching all time with amazement. I wasn't sure but had the feeling that Betty had figured all this out. I thought maybe I could ask her and she could explain it all to me.

June had made plans that would go ahead. June, Kayla and I were to go sailing on the "Cat." The "Cat," of course, was our 54 foot Hunter. June had planned this so that she and Kayla could get some one-on-one time with me.

The three of us would take two days and sail over to Harbor Island. We hadn't been over in a while, but Madilyn had kept up with bringing in a clean-up crew.

The sail over was great, Kayla now almost 5 can swim like a fish. June would put a top on her, and Kayla would throw it off. It was also hard keeping a life jacket attached to Kayla. The weather was good, and we arrived at Valentine's the following afternoon. We went straight to the house and walked over to the Pink Sands for dinner. The Kings were not there but one of the daughters had just graduated from college and took care of the business. The food and wine were as good as always. Our walk back had me carrying Kayla as she had a long day. The night on the beach with June went well with June not complaining about anything but the no see ums. It had been a while that I could recall not having something ruin the time I had at the Harbor Island House. Everything went as planned. I couldn't remember getting to sail there and back during the same trip; it was great.

On our forth day we were coming into the Nassau dock. Pete whom had caught the first line from the "Princes" was there to catch our bow line. Standing there with Pete was a welcoming party of ten. There were Johnny and Caroline, Melody, Michelle, Kelly, Jac,

Jim and of course the three musketeers Pearl, Sunshine, and Najima. Kayla was Anxious to get to the children as she had missed them so much. The youngest, little Jim, was screaming for his sister Kayla and his mama, June. It looked like Sunshine was the happiest to see us; she couldn't stop smiling.

In the old days, we couldn't have left the dock without stopping at the bar to see Willy. As we all walked by the bar, June having my one arm and Najima the other, June said, you miss him, don't you? My response was, yes, mam, him and all the others we've lost.

From there we all walked to Ms. Angee's restaurant, there another welcoming of us all. With our group, the restaurant was standing room only. It was Agee's first time meeting Najima; of course, Angee started telling stories about her meeting me on my first day on the Island and knowing all my girlfriends from the first to now. Angee now said that June was her favorite. I then acted surprised and said I thought her favorite was Michelle. Angee said that where men were concerned, Michelle was pure evil. Caroline then mentioned that Jena had been calling, saying I needed to call her back. Caroline said that when she told Jena that I was out fishing, Jena then asked for June. Caroline then said that she had told Jena that we would be returning today. Najima then asked, who's Jena? Angee said that she was the one that the house fell on in the movie. June laughed, and Najima asked, what movie? Angee then said, why the Wizard of OZ, of course. Najima said she must have missed that one. June said because it had come out before Najima was born. Pearl now at the restaurant, said that she had taken Najima for a ride in her T28. Pearl said she had never heard someone scream so loud. Najima said she wanted to vomit, but her stomach couldn't find her mouth. We all got a laugh out of that.

Melody then reminded me that it was time to go and bring back Gary, Joe-Anne, and Sam. We all miss them, Melody said. I agreed and said I would send the message to have them ready to be picked up on June first.

I didn't make it back to the Hill Top house that night. The girls had it all planned. Najima and I would be dropped off at the old beach house. The refrigerator had been stocked, and it looked like I would be cooking. It was the first time I had seen Najima in a bathing suit. Caroline had taken Najima shopping at both our tourist shops. What the two of them couldn't find at the stores, they borrowed from Lori's things. No one would have ever imagined what was under all those clothes. It made me think that maybe all Arab women looked so, which is why the men had them hiding. Lying on the beach, I got a glimpse of a mark that was peeking from under Najima's bathing suit bottom. The bottoms didn't cover much but high on her right thy there it was. I moved the suit bottom to get a better look. By touching the mark it seamed to be a scar of some kind, then looking closer I knew exactly was it was. It was a brand; the design matched the Medallion that I had taken from the skeleton that looked like their dead leader at the Oasis. I asked Najima when she received the mark, and she said that it was not a scar but a birthmark. This wasn't the time or place for this discussion. This was the time for some lessons. The girl couldn't swim.

I had started cooking dinner; I had fresh crawfish ready for the oven; I had split the crawfish and cleaned out the shell, all except the tail. I was boiling potatoes to make whipped potatoes to put that in the crawfish heads empty cavity then bake them. Things were looking good until Najima came walking out in one of my favorite nighties. Looking at her was all it took to cancel my cooking plans. Everything else in the kitchen was turned off.

It was the first time that Najima and I had been in a real bed together. Someone had added silk sheets. These could have even been the sheets that Deanna put on the front bunk of the "Johnny" on the day Deanna had turned 16. Way back then, Deanna, at 16, claimed she was then my woman. You see, Deanna's mom had deliverer Deanna's sister Wendy at that age.

Anyway, the sheets were nice, but what took the place of dinner would have been great served anywhere. The next morning I was up at 5:00 a.m.

I made my Cuban coffee and decided to open the safe and maybe read some of Michelle's diary. I thought I was sure of where Lori had put it. It was missing, and I was convinced that Lori must have returned and taken it from the safe. I wasn't mad but did want it put back where it belonged. On the safe's floor, I felt the sea bottoms sand with my bare feet. The sand between my toes brought back so many memories. I sat on the floor looking at old photos. There were photos of Michelle at age 12 until about when I first met her. I didn't hear Najima come in, but she was standing, looking over my shoulder. She was beautiful, Najima said. Yes, I said; I can still see her walking down that spiral staircase at the Governor's House in that red dress. In the old days, I said, Angee worked for Bob when he was in town. When Bob wasn't here, Angee had an old cart that she cooked and sold conch salad and crawfish fitters from, down by the docks. Betty also worked for Bob in those days. Betty mostly raised Michelle from age 12. Michelle had said she fell in love with Bob when she was 15. Bob invested in Michelle's future while Michelle, when Bob was away, made money working her beauty and men's lust for it. Michelle's diary was always here; it took me these many years to think I could read some of it. I told Najima that Lori must have it. Najima then asked out of the blue why I hadn't married June? That's a strange thing to ask, I said. Why Najima asked? At present, you only have me as your wife, and I don't mind if you have another. Soon I will bear us a child. June, Najima said is doing a good job of raising your children. While I'm fighting along your side, June will stay home and care for the children. Najima almost had me speechless. I thought about spanking her, but it just didn't work out that way.

I was thinking of taking Najima with me to General Santos. As it turned out, Pearl had plans to start teaching Najima to fly. Johnny was now teaching Caroline.

Having two sets of the card, keys were good but leaving one set with Pearl was a bit scary.

Pearl gave me her word not to even open the Vehicle's door while I was gone. Security was high.

General Santos now had a paved runway at it's airport. I planned to get in and out the same day. It would still be a long ride, this as we would have a C-130 tag along. The tag-along would include some supplies that Lori had requested plus a crew of the Black Devils to relive the ones that were there in General Santos working with Lori. I hoped the security men and two women were not working in the fields.

Before I had left for General Santos, I had gotten my kiss from June and my first I love you from Najima. Najima said if I decided to bring Lori back, she would be ok with it. Najima also said that it was Pearl that wanted Lori to return.

It was May 29th when we took off. It would be the first of June when when we set down in General Santos.

The tone at the airport was different, there were people there. There was another plane at what looked like a gateway. Best of all, Sam was there waiting! Running at me, Sam said he knew I would come for them. Sam had come with a company car with 4 of our Black Devils. The men said they also were glad to see me.

We drove straight to the house; the children were there waiting for their Papa; Chubby and Lilly said they would also return with the children. Gary and Joe-Anne had grown so. Lori was, of course, not at home, and Lilly said that Lori asked that I at least spend the night.

I asked Sam where I could find her; Sam said down at the docks as Lori's new ship was here making its third trip. Lilly said that Lori spent most of her time working.

As we arrived, I saw the port looked to be quite busy. When we found Lori, I got out of the car then, from a distance, watched her. Her hair had grown out long; she wore a wide brim hat, a short-sleeved shirt, work shorts, and high-top lace-up boots. She looked 20 or 30 pounds lighter. She was there giving orders, and the people were moving as she gave them. As I continued to watch, I was surprised by what looked like, and was a container crane being erected. The ship that was there alongside the dock was using its ship's crane to lift off the containers. The name on the ship's stern was "CARIBBEAN PEARL." The name had me walking toward Lori; when close enough that I thought she'd hear me, I gave out my whistle. Lori snapped around and came running. Right before she reached me she stopped. She looked at me and asked if it was for real or for show. Lori then looked over my shoulder, then back at me. I said that I was still in love with that skinny girl from the docks. Lori then walked the next few steps, took her hat and threw it on the ground, and came into my arms. With my kiss, Lori said that she still loved me just as much or more than ever. Then come home with me, I said. Lori smiled and said that she now understood why I worked as I have. No, she said I couldn't and won't give this up. I'll stay your wife and even give you more children if you want, I will remain loyal until you divorce me or one of us die, but here I will wait and build. Now she said, I have to get back to work; you will stay a few days? she asked? Please stay, she said.

I turned and told Sam to go to the house and find my work clothes and boots. Sam smiled as he turned, running toward the car.

When I turned, Lori had picked up her hat and was again giving orders.

From the ship I heard someone calling, Captain! I looked, and it was Nilo, calling from aboard. I walked to the ship's stairs and started up. At the top, I was stopped by security. Sorry sir the woman said, no visitors. Behind the woman was one of my oldest Black Devils; he then started laughing. I taught her good right, Captain? He said.

Nilo was now at where we were and, with a hug, said, welcome aboard, Captain.

Nilo said they were going out full, the other ships too he said, yes we have competition he said. But not to worry, Lori has more cargo than we can carry.

The fruit company and the tuna factory both give us freight. Lori's ship doesn't call the same ports as the others, he said with a smile.

Sam was soon at ship's side with my clothes, I went down and changed, then worked until the ship was loaded and was leaving the dock.

When Lori and I left the port, we were both tuckered out. I hadn't worked so hard since I could remember.

Once at home, it was to the shower, Lori had lost weight, but that shower was still as good as I could remember.

We had a late dinner, here we didn't have to bring sea food with us. No conch, but in its place was calamari. The prawns here were 4 to make the weight of a pound. The children stayed up until we all sat and ate. Sam had been busy working but had taken the time to ensure that Gary and Joe-Anne could swim like a fish. Both children could dive in and come up at the other side of the pool.

Sam wanted to hear of our latest adventure. Chubby wanted to hear about the war. Sam asked if it was true that Pearl was now an ace pilot? Gary wanted to know when he could get a ride in his sister's new jet? Lori quieted them all by asking how many new girlfriends I had? Gary and Joe-Anne both said, "daddy's in trouble."

Lori would not go to work the next day; she wanted to hear everything, including everything about the Prince's two-legged gift. Somehow I got through most of the story without getting into too much trouble, or at least I thought so.

When I got around asking about Michelle's diary, Lori said that she hadn't finished it. Lori said that she disagreed with how Michelle made her money but that Michelle knew how to keep it and make it grow. Lori asked just how much money Michelle had left me? Lori then mentioned that the new crane being built on the pier was ours, ours at the cost of over $4,000,000. I asked where the money had come from? Lori said that she had used some of her profits plus had given a 20-year lease on the property north of the Fish Factory. She went on to say that she then had the fruit company sign a five-year contract for crane services. I asked who had leased the land? Lori said Mr. Mitchocomi, the Japanese from the tuna factory. I then said they were not to be trusted. Lori said that their written agreement guaranteed that only 3 out of every 100 employees would be foreigners. I then said that the land she leased wasn't hers to lease. I will, I said, give them their money back. Lori said no. No, I said, you can't lease property that is not yours, I said. Yes, Lori said I can and I did. The property is in trust and I am the trustee Lori said. The trust takes two signatures; I said, yours and mine. Lori said that if the other required signature is out of the country for more than thirty days, I can and did. You could have contacted me, I said. And what would you have said Lori asked?

Your making decisions for me I said, you didn't ask. You hid this from me I said. Like Michelle did, Lori said. She hid things only to protect me, I said. No, Lori said she knew about the treasure; when she gave you the money for the boat, she knew the treasure was down there. No way, I said. Yes, Lori said that Michelle had written in her diary that the King Fish had told her that he had found a treasure and that if she left Bob, he would share it with her. Michelle wrote that when you came and met with Bob telling him that you knew where the treasure was, that she decided then that she would use you to get to the treasure. I don't believe you I said. The diary Lori said, read it yourself.

My stomach turned; I started to walk out of the room, turned, and asked for the diary. Once in hand, I turned, walked out to the indoor balcony, and yelled to Chubby below, "get everyone together; we are leaving here in twenty minutes."

I then walked down the stairs and located Gary and Joe-Anne. Come children; we are going home, I said. I looked up the stairs, and there stood Lori. Wave goodbye to your mother I said. Both waved, and each threw her a kiss.

It took a little longer than I wanted to get off the ground. At the airport, there was a hold-up; the new airport also had an immigration person that at first refused to permit Gary and Joe-Anne to board the Leer. I ordered the C-130 to lift off, with TESS in the air and eight heavily armed Black Devils standing with me; I then changed our destination with the immigration from Nassau to Manila. At first, the immigration person also refused this option. General Santos airport was supported by two police and two military personnel. All 4 were then relieved of their arms and radios. The phone line was also cut. I then thanked all the people for their cooperation, and we all boarded the Leer and took off without further delay.

It wasn't what Lori said about Michelle, or the money, or the lease. It was how she said it and did it. She was signing a paper for 20 years when all she had to do was to ask for the money. I was sure that Lori had called the airport to slow us down until she could get some kind of paper hold on the children. What seemed to be a good beginning between Lori and I sure went sour fast.

For the first few hours of the trip home, I thought about how I might slow Lori's financial progress. Then it all hit me, Lori had done what I taught her to do so well. She turned out just like me. What would she do when I didn't return with the children?

As the Leer was landing at the Nassau airport, the pilot reported that the Prince's two planes were parked there. We had earlier contact with June, but she made no mention of any visitors. Air traffic over Haiti was a different story. Pearl had reported that so much air and sea traffic were cramping her style. Najima's flying lessons had been put on hold as the Paxi base had been on constant alert.

Once at the house, June said she had only seen Najima once since I had left. June mentioned that Sunshine, too was now stationed on Paxi.

June said that she was made aware of the Prince's visit this morning just hours before we had arrived.

I called for Najima to let her know that the Leer would be on the way to pick her up, but while making the call, Najima was walking in the Hill Top front door. There was no apology from Najima to June for the kiss Najima gave me. It seemed the tide had somewhat changed. Najima then came and also kissed June, Najima calling June big sister. I imagined that Pearl had spoken to Lori, Lori letting Pearl know that we had parted on not-so-good terms, Pearl passing that along to Najima.

I asked Najima to contact the Prince, and let's get this meeting over with.

I then went into the office and put a call into the Admiral. My call did not go through; I was sure he had given orders not to put my call through until I called the second or third time. Jack was on home time on Eleuthera, and Dan was at the moment controlling our air space. I spoke with Dan telling him to get the two new C-130s in the air and show our Paxi area's visitors some of our new tricks. Dan knew exactly what I was talking about. I then sent a coded message to Lourdes that she was urgently to send the Admiral. The message would read, "Admiral, the northwest of Haiti is experiencing difficulties with navigational and electrical instrumental as well as communication blockage between vessels and aircraft, please advise all ships and aircraft within the triangle."

It wasn't 15 minutes after that message went out that we got a call from the Admiral. Captain, he asked, how have you been? Get to the chase I said. We need to meet he said. What is the topic I asked? Airpower, the Admiral said, you've got it. We want it. I didn't hesitate, "you shot down a civilian plane with 11 civilians aboard I said. I have it on video and camera satellite. Nine of those killed were American citizens. What do you say to that claim Admiral", I asked? The Admiral then said he had an inbound call he must take and for me to standby. I knew the call must be coming from their carrier sitting only 20 miles north of the Paxi coastline. We had two of our C-130s up there with TESS messing with navigation, electrical, and now even their communications. Yes TESS could now cut communications between fighters and or the carrier from which they had taken off from. The Admiral was back on the phone and demanded that we release our hold on his assets. If you are speaking of my message about what we are experiencing in the triangle, this phenomenon has been coming and going long before we met. Today is the worse we experienced in years I said. The Admiral said that the carrier had called its fighters back, but it seemed that there was a communication block. How many are out on patrol I asked? The Admiral then said that they had five fighters unaccounted for. What about your satellites I asked? Can't they locate the fighters? I then said that I would meet him and the director on Eleuthera in three days at 0800 hours on the tarmac. Bring your most advanced pilot, I said. One copter, unarmed. The Admiral said they'd be there. Now he said can you assist with my fighters before they run out of fuel he asked? Maybe it's that large piece of metal that messing with things. If I were you, I'd try heading it further to the north I said. See you Eleuthera he said.

As I got off the call, I contacted Dan. Free them up so they can return to their ship, I said; if the carrier doesn't head north, give them some of the same. Dan said that already one aircraft had ditched, and he wasn't sure if the others could make it back to the ship without doing the same. Did the pilot make it out I asked? Dan said yes and that he would pass on the GPS coordinates of the down pilots once their ship could receive them. Dan then, with that voice of his, asked if he should warn them of the sharks?

The carrier turned north, but still, they lost two of their fighters to the Caribbean Sea. They suffered no lost of life.

The Prince was contacted and would visit the Hill Top house after their evening prayers.

He didn't seem upset, as once he entered the house, I handed him their set of card keys. I told him that my decision to pull out was base on his request to move both Vehicles to Riyadh, but the deal changer was his troop movement toward our location. I trust our pulling out has saved our relationship I said. The Prince smiled and asked about training a group of his pilots. I offered that once I had three capable pilots that I would send them one. Your daughter Pearl he said, we would like her to train our pilots. I'll speak with her I said, maybe if Najima went along, Pearl just might agree. Yes of course, by all means send them both. Najima will always be welcome in our house, the Prince said.

Now then the Prince said, the King would like to buy back the two C-130s that he gave to you; of course, the King would want the TESS program to accompany the planes. The king, the Prince said, has sent with me with an offer of $200,000,000 each. Tell the king that his offer is most generous and I will think it over during the next several months. The Prince smiled and said yes, of course. Before the Prince left, he turned and said that if it were necessary to match another offer, he would consider it.

When the Prince finally left it was after 9:00 p.m. The children had gone to bed, but June and Najima were still up and waiting. I asked June to have the house girl make me a bed out on the porch. The bed was made up and I would retire there. Both June and Najima joined me on the porch. It looked like we all were going to sleep on the porch, so I got up and headed to June's room. Both girls followed. It just didn't feel right. I felt good with June and also with Najima but not together. Not to hurt one or the other, I would go sleep with Gary. I woke the next morning with Najima sleeping alongside Gary's bed on the floor. I got up, scooped her up, and put her in bed with Gary. Then went into the kitchen to find my coffee ready. Betty, whom I thought must be well into her seventies, asked if I was also ready for some of her pancakes? The yes please, coming from behind me, was from Najima. Najima now had on a pair of tight fitting jeans a black satin top without braw or her typical black headgear. You did not sleep well my husband Najima asked? How about a sail this morning I asked? After pancakes or before, she asked? After, June answered as she walked in. Breakfast for three I said. The sailing invitation is for both wives, or just one June asked?

It was mid-June, and out on the porch, the cool air from the kitchen's open door cooled the muggy morning. I looked north, then out to the east seeing the sun just peeking up. I will take you both, I said, but all must be comfortable with it, including me. No competition I said. You both pack a small bag and wear what you want. The sun will be bright and hot today; in two days, we will meet visitors for business on Eleuthera, then spend a few days on Harbor Island before the two of you will sail back alone. If you both can't get along as my companions, I will then pick a wife. June spoke first, so if we get along together, you will only have two wives? Yes, I said, just like when Lori was here with us. No visits to Miami to see Kay, June asked? If I visit Kay, one of you will go with me.

Before leaving Hill Top I sent instructions for my meeting with the Admiral and the Director.

The three of us then left the house for Nassau's city dock. The "CAT" was there waiting for us. June had grabbed a few things from the house that, along with whatever I'd catch, would complete our meals.

The day was beautiful as was my company. We motored out the channel then while I showed Najima how to hold the wheel into the wind, June went forward and raised the main. Once she returned to the cockpit, June pulled back the jib line, which brought it to life. I then turned the wheel and the wind caught both sails. June used the winch on the jib, and I pulled in the main sheet line. As I had said many times, the Hunter was built for this; she was sleek, built for speed, she was comfortable but not built for comfort. The wind's direction would not allow us a direct line of travel, and we would not reach where I wanted to be for the night. I hadn't trolled off a sailboat since I was a kid crossing the Gulf Stream with Rusty on the "Princess." I rigged a line and found a nice trolling spool. It wasn't long until we had caught dinner. I sailed, and the girls cooked.

We didn't reach a safe place to anchor until about 1:00 a.m. Once anchored and the boat all buttoned up, the three of us hit the front cabin without problems. It seemed our little conversation had worked.

The next morning after coffee I was overboard getting crawfish and even a few conch. My favorite food is cooked and chilled crawfish, placed in a ziplock with a squeezed lime. June did her best at conch fritters, but I ended up doing the cooking. The best fitter cooking was, of course, done by Angee or my Uncle Bob. With Angee or my Uncle, all the fixens were fresh, and neither wanted help in the kitchen.

We had ready breakfast and lunch. Yesterday the girls dressed for the sun. This morning they both wore what I liked. I wasn't sure if it was underwear or a bathing suit bottom and a "T" shirt. Even living in the Bahamas, June's skin was light while Najima's, even though she had some of that soft skin mix somewhere in her genes, her skin was that Brownish Arab silky smooth tan. The day would be another all Sun. We scooped up seawater and poured it over us to keep cool. By late afternoon we arrived at Valentine's. We docked then took a cab to the house. We would have dinner at the Pink Sands, then walk home, stepping over the tiny turtles making their first trip to the sea.

CHAPTER XVI

THE TEST FLIGHT

THE NEXT MORNING WE STARTED early as we would be having our little meeting with the Admiral. The Airport on Eleuthera was small, but Jack had ensured we would have the space we needed for our meeting to include a small show. The Admiral's copter showed on time; Dan was in the air, Jack was with me, as we're June and Najima. Maria was somewhere there, close enough if she was needed.

The copter was shut down, and everyone was introduced. Both the Admiral and the Director had met June, but neither had met Najima. Jack they knew of but also had not met. I had a long history with the Admiral and knew the Director as well. It was our first meeting with their pilot. As we said hello, Pearl would appear and land her Harrier. I asked the pilot if he could fly her? The pilot said he could fly anything that was made to fly. We'll see, I said. I then asked the seasoned pilot if he minded wearing two bracelets made up for him? The pilot asked what the bracelets were for? I said the bracelets were to monitor his heart plus, more importantly, were a deterrent from him taking the jet with him without Pearl's permission. You have heard the expression "it cost an arm and a leg," I asked? The pilot looked at me and said Yes, Sir.

The Pilot looked at the Admiral, the Admiral nodding his approval. Jack placed one strap on the Pilot's right arm then one on his left leg. As we walked toward the jet, the built-proof glass hood popped open and out stepped Pearl. Good morning Pearl said. Pearl looking at the Pilot, said to climb on up. The pilot went up, and Pearl followed, remaining on the wing. Pearl showed the pilot a few things, including the laser gun that was installed just over the noise of the jet. Pearl told him that the Harrier's black look was not paint but the natural color of the new material made up to replace the many parts that had been changed. The new material she said, was lighter and stronger plus after adding a small electrical charge would allow the Harrier to all but disappear from most radars to include make it hard for even satellites to see. It will run on ordinary jet fuel, but today, the power has been modified. The fuel has a super-charged octane that has an additive that allows a higher heat tolerance. There is no war payload aboard except the small laser with two degrees of power, shooting two different rays. Today's flight only has the lighter side of what we call the blinder. Should you hit an object with this Ray, the laser should take out any visual that your opponent may have. The stealth power at this point only works the radar and does not affect the visible. Now you are ready; please remember that my father will not hesitate to destroy this jet with you in it. Your today's limit on range is at 150 miles. Before you start, you will be required to say out loud the pledge to our flag before starting your take-off. This Pearl said it will allow TESS to identify your voice commands. Pearl then dropped to the ground and started backing toward us.

While Pearl had given the pilot instructions, Jack had set up a small table with a large umbrella. Jack put on the table a large brief case. He then opened it and pushed the button on. As the computer and screens came on, we heard the pilot saying the pledge to allegiance, first speaking in English, then the voice, his voice switched to speaking Russian. The Admiral then quickly noted that their pilot didn't speak Russian. Pearl, now being with us, said that the voice we were hearing speaking Russian was that of TESS. Yes, Pearl said that TESS could mimic any voice and change the language.

The engines started and the jet then took off. Jack's computer showed the airport's radar plus the above satellite coverage. Pearl put on a head set that allowed her communication with the pilot. Show us what you have, Major, she said. The jet took off to the north then came back around. Pearl told the Major to switch on the electric current. As the pilot did what Pearl had told him to, the Harrier disappeared from the briefcase's radar images.

Pearl then activated the tracer bands that the pilot was wearing. Now we could see where the jet was. Jack had arranged for the Eleuthera air tower to be empty of personnel and had set up cameras pointing out in each direction. The pilot was to come around now and target the tower with the low-powered laser beam. From our spot at the end of the runway, Jack brought up the four-tower cameras' live viewing. The Harrier went out 5 miles, then coming in at our backs, targeted and fired on the tower. Just before the jet fired its laser, the tower's north pointing camera picked up the approaching plane, then went blank as the plane approached and passed overhead. Not just the north-facing camera went blank; they all did. The pilot was then asked to return and land.

The Director spoke first; he asked if any of this technology had come from our most recent find? Pearl answered, saying that the only thing we used from our trip was to change the engine's filtering capacity for the desert sands. So you're telling us that this same technology you have here the U.S. government received at the same time you did, but you did something with it, but our government didn't. I then looked at the two of them and said, no sir. Your opportunity had a good 25 years head start.

What about the new Vehicle, the Admiral asked? The vehicle has not yet been fully explored, I said. Our protocol Harrier does not have a TESS computer aboard; the Harrier only has a direct line of communication with TESS. TESS, as we call it, is still something that needs more understanding. More than the present administration appears to have, I said.

The pilot had now landed and was now with us. The Admiral asked what he thought? The pilot with the rank of Major asked what had happened in the tower? The Admiral said that its visual had been disabled. The Major asked about the radar? The Admiral said that we had only picked up his security bands. The Major then said it was the most remarkable piece of equipment he had ever flown. To fly without being detected or targeted by radar changes our adversary's ability to track our movements or fire their rockets at us. What about satellites picking up the Harrier, the Major asked? I then said that the electrolyzed jet parts fool the radar, but a satellite could still photograph the jet's movements. That's where TESS could one day assist I said. TESS can disrupt the satellite's ability to send or receive data, including photos. The Major then admitted that his prior experience with TESS was not good.

By now, Pearl had returned to and re-boarded the jet. Pearl then took off upward, then straight out to sea; she then returned, making a low altitude pass by while rolling around and around.

The Major switched his question about Pearl, how long has she been flying, he asked? She started at a young age; her toys have always been things like a T-28, of which she has two. She should join the Air Force he said. I then mentioned that she didn't do well following orders.

The Major then asked if the low-level laser could damage a pilot's eyesight? I said that the low-level laser could temporarily blind the pilot or anyone with whom the laser came in direct contact. We have not tested long-term eye damages, I said. We have, however, produced a lens that, when used in a pilot's headgear, the laser's flash only makes a moment of the closing of the pilot's eyes, taking only seconds for the eyes to recover fully. Of course, in a dog fight, a few seconds could mean life or death. The Major wanted to know when they could get their hands on a few of our Harriers? I looked at the Admiral and said that would be up to them. I'm not against our government; the problem is, they want things their way. TESS is a good example I said. I have told them repeatedly that TESS is not ready to be used by the military. The Major asked why and how was it that I had so much success with its use? It's a mutual thing, I said. I respect TESS and it in turn, TESS respects me. Are you saying that TESS actually thinks? Yes Sir, I said, TESS sees anything that is armed as a threat. When we started, TESS fired without warning. At present with development, if you come to close, close enough to fire at TESS, TESS will now warn that you are not welcome in its airspace. If TESS felt another aircraft posed a threat, it could then feel the need to remove the threat. It will be years before TESS is ready for use by the military, I said.

The Harrier, I said, is a simple tool that can be used to save our pilot's lives. We only ask that our government backs off while we continue with development. Please understand, Major, all of this technology was at one time handed over to our government. At a cost of much less than a new carrier, the technology information provided to the government could have been developed into what I have today and much, much more. The way the present government works, building a new carrier spreads the pork. The government still thinks it's easier to steal the developed technology and not wait until safe to use. TESS is a prime example, I said.

I looked at the three of them and asked, will you back off? The Major asked, can we trust you? I pointed at the straps on his arm and leg. You already have, I said. Tell you what I said, how many of these Harriers would you buy. The Admiral then said that they had purchased several TESS units with terrible results. Again I said that I had warned that TESS was not ready, but you went ahead anyway. The Director then spoke for the first time. How much time will you need to have the Harriers ready? With payment for the losses your carelessness caused and an agreement on price, six months to a year I said. The Harriers will be built in the U.K. I said. The U.K. will also have the same equipment. Balance of power I said. And the Saudis the Admiral asked? They, as I do, have a fully working vehicle, I said. The King has little patience and no pilots. The Admiral didn't say it, but I knew he thinking it. I then said that it would be a heavy price to pay, one way or another. You could do it, the Admiral said. You could easily have taken them both. Here we go again I said, looking at the Director.

The Pilot's bracelets had been removed, and he thanked us for the ride. The Pilot asked what the possibility was that he get the chance to fly the Vehicle. Good at Video games, sir, I asked?

The group of three then re-boarded their copter and were off to return to Washington. June, Najima, and I would return to Harbor Island via the ferry. Jack was only minutes from his and Cindy's home on Eleuthera.

Once back on Harbor Island, I decided the three of us would make ready and sail back to Nassau. June and Najima seemed to be getting on as sisters, Najima said that June was the number one wife, and she, Najima was the number two. Najima at least showed no jealousy at all. Both girls looked great in a bathing suit. Najima had now learned the sailing basics but asked, with all the technology that we had, why the toilet was so behind the times?

CHAPTER XVII

THE SOVIETS MOVE

WE WOULD REACH NASSAU THE following evening just in time to see the last of our crawfish boats come in.

Pearl had run a little experiment using her bracelet and took me behind the office's closed door to tell me about what she had found. TESS would not fire on the bracelet. This information made me think that I should have removed all the bracelets from the dead at the Oasis. In asking TESS about the bracelets and their protection use, TESS informed me that the bracelet's protection output could be overridden, but it was all or nothing. In other words, the protection of a TESS regulated firing could be overridden, but if overridden, all would then be vulnerable to being targeted by TESS. These bracelets TESS informed were not made here on earth and were meant to be passed along from generation to generation.

I didn't think for a moment that the Saudis wouldn't use the key cards and have one of their pilots attempt to fly and or at least test the laser weapons that were aboard. In my asking Pearl what she thought about the possibility of the Saudis flying their Vehicle, Pearl repeated that only someone that had flown one before, such as

Maximus, would be able to pilot that Vehicle. Pearl said that much like the Donzi, the Vehicle had little brakes. Pearl then admitted that not too long ago, she and Johnny had hit and damaged both the boat's bow and the dock. Pearl said that the Donzi's reverse's thrust just wasn't enough of a match with their forward motion. I looked surprised, and Pearl laughed as I hadn't heard about that accident before now.

Pearl said that it wouldn't be long now before Mr. Rodger's ship was ready for a trial flight. Pearl mentioned that the ship that Mr. Rodgers was building was in the class of the brothers Orville's and Wilbur's first flight. It took the brothers years to develop their flying machine, she said. I wonder, she said, what the next 50 years will bring. She then said that she hoped that we wouldn't have to look for another home by then, but if we do, we'll at least be ready. I sure hope that place has crawfish and conch, I said. Pearl then came and hugged me, as she had never done until now.

Maximus, I said, I want to speak with Maximus; we must find him. I wanted to find out what Maximus was up to. I felt that Maximus must now know, if not before now, what had taken place with the site find at the Oasis and that we, including the Saudis, have a working Vehicle. If Maximus didn't indeed have the first Vehicle, he now knew where there were two others. If Maximus did have the first Vehicle and Eorum thought he did not, Maximus, long before knew that the first Vehicle's control board had been modified. The modification had taken place due to the Israelis stealing one little part; the original controller had back then overheated, requiring G.D. to rebuild it. If Maximus hadn't already, I felt that he would contact the Saudis. If so, I felt that once he got in their Vehicle, he could somehow attempt to steal the vehicle from them.

Pearl and I had been alone while discussing Pearl's experiment and Maximus. Najima was patiently waiting outside the door. As Pearl walked out, she took Najima by the arm and said her vacation was over. Najima looked at me over her shoulder as Pearl pulled on her. I heard Pearl say, "back to classes, little sister." Pearl then looked back and said that Sunshine was spending her days in the front seat of a T28 with Johnny in the back seat; she added that I was falling behind. Pearl was of course, speaking of my flying lessons. My thoughts were that one air crash had been enough.

It was later that night when Jerry called on an open line alerting me that the fourth and final Navy man had been located. This was the last of four who years ago had attacked Lucy and killed Carla on Andros. This time we would involve Carla's sister, who was still working with our Black Devil Group. Shirley and Maria would be informed, and Jerry would set a plan in motion. The Navy man had been in jail for an unrelated crime, serving a 10-year sentence. Henry had been paroled for good behavior. If we could have been at his parole hearing, it wouldn't have gone so well for him. If Henry knew where he was going from his State's side jail, he just might have chosen to stay put in the prison he was in. This time it wouldn't be so easy as the last time when Evette and Christina nabbed their man in New Orleans. This time Henry was now living in a small town that didn't even have an airport. Henry was now working in a chicken farm, going to work, then straight home except paydays. Payday was the only time Henry might do some shopping or take in a movie. Jerry's plan involved having Henry's old pick-up not start as he came out of the show. Shirley would be there offering Henry a ride. The door handles all except Shirley's, would be spiked with my unique mix that could quickly render Henry unconscious. Maria would be close behind with a van that would follow Shirley and, by then, the unconscious Henry until they came to a good spot. One of our helicopters would be waiting and fly the three of them to the nearest airport that could handle one of Jerry's C-130s. From there, Henry's next stop would be Nassau, where Lucy would be waiting when the ramp came down.

That night didn't end there; June and I were in the shower when one of the house girls opened the bedroom door and, almost at a yell, said there was an urgent phone call. As I opened the glass shower door, I could see my radio's red light blinking. Exiting the shower I picked up the radio and phone line. On the line was Dan; Pearl's T28 had been shot down over open waters, and we hadn't received any word of survivors. The information was sketchy but what we knew was that Pearl was flying south heading to Paix and heard a mayday call from a ship that claimed to be on fire and sinking. Pearl radioed that she was going to take a flyover. Within moments Pearl radioed that she had the burning ship in her sights and would fly by and take a closer look. That was Pearl's last transmission, except they had heard Pearl tell Najima that they were going down. Yes, Najima was with Pearl. Dan said that everything we had was in the air and that we now had at least one GPS responder sounding. Dan reported that the ship that had been burning could have sunken as our radar had picked it up, then it disappeared. Our one C-130 with the two super radar equipment was now off the ground from Paix and would be within tracking range in minutes. Our two helicopters at Paix were also dispatched. Dan then said that the one GPS signal that we did have had stopped putting out its signal. I said to drop life rafts at the last ping. Dan said that we already had two manned rafts in the water with more on the way.

Within minutes, our super radar had picked up a submarine in the same area where that last ping had come from. I ordered that if the sub surfaced, it would be disabled, not sunk. I had never felt so helpless; all I could do was to wait.

I put a call into the Admiral's home number; he grumbly answered the phone. I made him aware of what was going on, and asked for any information he might have of any Russian Navy in the area. It wouldn't be daylight for another 4 or 5 hours; the Admiral said he would alert the Coast Guard from Miami, them possibly sending several cutters and a set of copters on out to Andros. I was good with that for now. I mentioned that his people should respect that 100-mile mark. Yes yes, of course, he said.

Dan said that TESS had warned the Russian sub to sit still; the submarine had just surfaced. The sub's commander said his vessel was in recovery mode as they had surfaced to assist a burning vessel and that a plane had passed by very low and caught fire from an explosion from the burning ship right before it had sunk. Of course, Dan wasn't buying any of that. It was dark, and Dan said we now had four motorized crafts in the water, but the super radar C-130 picked up six such vessels. It was at this point that Dan had decided to take out the sub's ability to propel, which would take away the sub's ability to dive and or move on its power.

Dan was in the process of doing just that, but a third party was now attacking the Sub. Dan's radar never even saw the attacker. From the Sub, a short Radio transmission said that they were under attack, ordering all measures to respond. Dan said that the skyward view showed the Sub's control tower in flames and parts of its deck on fire. There was now three sections on fire from the sub. Radio transmission from the Sub had suddenly stopped.

Dan said that GPS ping of ours now started pinging again.

I was back on the phone with the Admiral informing him on what was going on. I explained that our group had not fired on the Sub. My call with the Admiral was interrupted with the news that one of our rescue crafts had picked up one of the girls. Pearl was; she had been floating in the ocean watching the entire show. Our men on the raft said that they were led to Pearl by a light coming down from the sky. That light was now moving, and one of our other rafts was on the way following. Dan said Pearl's only concern was for Najima, who had not seen or heard her calls since hitting the water. Pearl had turned off her GPS ping when seeing the sub launch their two rubber boats. Pearl said that seeing the Sub's tower searchlight, she had turned off her ping as she knew they were looking for Najima and herself. The report was that Pearl was ok but had not seen Najima. Not two minutes later, the search team reported having Najima aboard one of our crafts; she was alive but had suffered several injuries. Najima had made it to one of our rafts that were dropped but was now not conscious. Both girls would now have been picked up by one of our copters and heading to Nassau's hospital. Not knowing of Najima's condition was no less than terrible. June, up and dressed, we headed on over to the hospital.

Dan now reported via radio that the copter with the girls aboard was heading to the Nassau hospital with an ETA of 30 minutes.

The Sub's fires now appeared to be under control with it still smoking. Our other copter was now overhead broadcasting through an auto system that was speaking Russian using TESS as the translator. Our copter was offering help with any wounded. The Subs deck was full of standing men with several injured being attended to on the deck.

Dan had contacted the U.S. Coast Guard requesting their assistance. It would still be another two hours before the Coast Guard could show. Our copter had lowered their stretcher and would carry four badly injured Russians toward Nassau.

At the hospital, our helicopter had arrived carrying the girls. Pearl had been treading water with a broken left arm plus small cuts and bruises. Pearl wouldn't leave Najima's side. From what we could see of Najima's injuries, she had a compound fracture of her left leg and possibly either a broken upper left shoulder or at least some damage there. The Doctors said that they were worried only about any internal injuries that Najima might have.

It would be two hours or more when Najima came out of surgery. The Good Doctors said that Najima had also suffered a badly bruised left kidney, along with four broken ribs a partially torn rotor cuff, and they had removed her spleen and repaired her damaged left leg. Besides these injuries and being quite beat up, she would recover just fine.

By now, the first group of injured Russians had arrived. What we got out of them was that the Sub had lost it's Captain as he was on the bridge at the time of the attack. The survivors said that all deck personnel had been killed; they didn't know how many that was.

Cuba sent out a tug that would tow the damaged Sub into a Cuban port. As the sun came up, additional U.S. Coast Guard helicopters arrived and picked up other injured from the Sub and would take them on to Cuba.

It turned out there was no burning sinking ship; the Russians had set the fire on their deck, them making the Mayday calls.

All approaching flights were sternly warned not to enter the 100 mile no-fly zone. Only rescue helicopters were permitted in. The remainder of the Sub's crew were mostly seated on deck. Food and supplies were dropped in.

It was at this point; we were sure of what we had thought. What ever it was, it had fired on the Sub. Only its lights were seen leading our people to both Pearl and Najima. We could only guess that it was Maximus that had come to the girls rescue. But where had he come from? How did he manage to get there so quickly?

Russia had now put in their highest protests claiming that their Sub was attacked while attempting to rescue the burning ship then the fallen T-28. The U.S. justifiably claimed it had no military presents in the area.

In all, Russia had lost 14 of their crew with 18 wounded, two that were critically burned and could go either way. Cuba had sent in 4 of their burn Doctors to over see the many with burns. We would watch the Doctors closely not permitting them to cross the bridge to Paradise Island. The Cuban government complained, and the Doctors, even the ones with the military, were given free rein of both Nassau and the Island.

The next morning Najima came too. Still in shock at what had happened. Najima remembered flying over the burning ship, then nothing. Najima asked the nurse if she had been pregnant? The nurse said luckily; she had not been. The nurse said that if she had been that the baby would not have survived. Pearl looked at me and said she, too, was not pregnant. Pearl thought it funny, I did not. Najima wanted to go home; the Doctor said the salt air out on the porch would do her good.

At home on the Island, Pearl and I plotted out the possibilities of how Maximus learned what was happening and got there so fast. We tried to use TESS but we mainly got resistance with TESS saying some things better not discussed. It wasn't a matter of distance, we didn't know the speed of his ship, we only knew that it was more than the 1,000 mph mark. I mentioned that I believed that the gold bracelet might have had something to do with it all. Maybe somehow, it put out a distress signal. Had TESS not been watching over the girls, even we wouldn't have known. Sunshine's room was now being set up to receive Najima; Sunshine was here at the Hill Top House and said she would be the one to care for Najima. Pearl said that if TESS had not been up there, she didn't think Najima would have made it, and she would have ended up aboard the Russian sub. Pearl asked why her? What would the Russians want with her? To steal the Saudi's Vehicle, one would need a pilot. Having a pilot and a hostage could have worked out well for the Russians.

I then said that Maximus would now have to move toward the Saudis quickly. The next step for the Russians would be to convince the Saudis that one of their cosmonauts could fly their Vehicle. No, I said Maximus will now go to the Saudis.

We still didn't know what Maximus would do with the Vehicle, we had no idea how he thought. Once he had such a power then what? Us warning the Saudis would do no good as they would think; if we wanted to help them, we could send Pearl. To warn them against Maximus would damage any possibility of getting closer to Maximus. What we would do was to start again testing the Vehicle that we did have.

The Russian Sub took two more days to arrive in Cuba. Cuba had two such Submarine basis that the Soviets had built during the height of the Cold War. The submersible sonar Vessels that Joe and I had built in the Seventies were constructed and used to detect the Soviets Submarines going in and out of Cuba. That I knew of, at least two of those same sonar vessels were still down there working. If working, the U.S. would have known that this sub was down there and for how long. It wasn't by chance that Russian sub was sitting there at that time. The Sub would have to have good intel that informed the Sub when Pearl took off. This meant that the Soviets had to have boots on the ground here in Nassau or at least the Nassau airport. If the U.S. knew the sub was down there, they should have figured why and alerted us. Why would the U.S. want to assist the Russians. My thoughts turned to Nassau, if they were on the Island, we would find them.

The next day Najima came home. Najima's leg cast wasn't a walking cast as Lori's had at one time been. Najima's cast was from her ankle to the top of her thy and bent back at the knee. This cast was open where the surgery had taken place. When Lori had on her cast, she was quite mobile; Najima would not be. I thought, a one legged shower? No a shower with crutches and a plastic bag.

Our intel wasn't very good as today Lori jetted in on us. As Pearl reminded me, Lori's and my divorce wasn't completed as yet. Pearl must have known that Lori was on the way as Pearl had taken Gary and Joe-Anne to the airport to meet Lori's plane. Lori came straight to Hill Top, only bringing a small handbag and gifts for the children, all of them. Damn, she looked as good as I could remember. From the children it was hugs with June and Betty, a small kiss on the cheek for me. From there, it was straight in to see Najima. As I followed close behind, Lori shut the door with me on the outside. I thought that Najima would have had a much better chance if she could have been on her feet.

While Lori and Najima talked, I had a talk with Pearl. Why I asked her? Pearl said that when Lori had heard about what had happened, she wanted to come to talk with me and pick up the children. Pearl said that Gary had told her that he would not return to General Santos, that Papa said he and Joe-Anne didn't have to go back. Pearl looked at me and said that I was their father but that I should not forget that Lori was their mother. Pearl said she would not choose between the two. Pearl looking at me, asked, why not forgive her and take her back? I have spoken to Najima she said. Pearl said that Najima was good with Lori coming back being a part of the family. Pearl said that Najima would be continuing with her flight training starting tomorrow, no not in the cockpit but with TESS here in my office. Pearl then informed me that she would not be tricked again by the Russians nor anyone. She said that her and Mr. Rodgers had designed a two-seat fighter that had the characters of the Harrier, not needing a runway that could be used with a TESS type modular that could coordinate with the Vehicle and our C-130s. That sounds like an offensive measure, I said. Pearl said that her family's passive attitude had gotten them to where they were today. The Russians and any other group must know that a stunt like the Russian Sub will not go unpunished. Killing 14 of the crew including their Captain and almost destroying their Sub wasn't punishment, I asked? No Pearl said that was only coming to the rescue, the bare minimum, I would say.

At this point of the conversation Lori came out from Sunshine's room. Before going into what you women have decided, I said I would like to speak with Najima first, alone, I said.

I then walked to Najima, swooping her off her bed. I asked Pearl to open the porch door, and as she did, I carried Najima out. Najima opened the outside screen door, and we went out and down the stairs. To the sand down by the where the small waves were breaking, still holding her, I put her down with her touching her right barefoot to the sand. I then asked if she was in love with me or was what we had, her playing the part of a King's gift? May I express my emotions, my husband, she asked? Yes I said. Najima then hugged me and kissed me, saying that I was her whole world; she loved me with all her heart and would until her last breath. I will not accept whatever Lori had talked her into, I said. I don't even want to hear it. I would like to hear what you would like to see happening with me telling you that I, too, am in love with you! June, I said, would most likely accept Lori coming back or whatever

Lori cooked up. June loves and cares for the children. As I have said before, June stays and is the number one wife. You are the number two wife but my number one love. You do not have to continue to master flying; you can stay at home or work at my side. I do not want to lose you to an air crash, nor some plan of Lori's or anything else that would separate us.

Now with all that said, Lori can come and go as she pleases. Gary and Joe-Anne will stay until the last day of August. Until school age, they will spend three months there, then three months here with us. Lori can do the same if she wishes to be with the family. If I may ask, you will not sleep in her bed Najima asked? You may ask anything from me; you are my wife. The answer is no; I more than once told Lori that I would never leave her. That it would be her doing the leaving. I am not now upset with her, and we all should treat her like family. I will not sleep in her bed nor she mine. Lori will at some time remarry; that man will not be family nor welcome at our home or table. What about me having children Najima asked? There will be plenty of time for children, I said; we should have at least two or three-four toes around the house, I said. Now give me that big kiss, and I'll cart you back up. Najima kissed me, and then, as I said, I carried her back up to the house. I looked at Lori and said that if she had any plans to take the children, they could leave on the last day of August. I don't want them to leave, but if they must, then that's when they can go. I told Lori that she was welcome to stay just as long as the children were here. I also stipulated that about the every three months thing and school. Lori then said that she didn't think that her children were safe here with me. I told her that the children being with her in General Santos made them a much easier target for someone to get to me. I looked right at her and told her that they all would be safer here in Nassau or Paix. What about us Lori asked? We are family; you are the mother of my children. We will not be lovers. June hearing the conversation asked if she could have input here? Yes, you should tell their mother how much her children love it here with their brother and sisters. If you're going to say that you don't mind sharing me, then don't. June then said that she needed more not less time with me. June said that her only worry was what would happen to the family if she lost me.

I held out my arms, and June came to me.

Lori's look was that of complete surprise. She called Gary and Joe-Anne and hugged them goodbye and told them that she would be back at the end of August to fetch them.

Lori then looked at me and said that I had promised her that I would always love her, but I had lied. I looked at Lori and told her that I would love her until the day that I died. You left this house and tried to block my children from going with me from the Philippines. I also understand that the divorce papers arrived were drawn up after Brian had rendezvoused with you in Manila. What Brian wants you, but without the children? Sounds familiar, I said. Again you are welcome here because of the children; there will be no talk of this after today, I said.

Pearl being there in the room, asked Lori if it was confirmed that she had met Brian in Manilla? Lori did not answer. Pearl waited a second then looking at Lori used the word Proditor, then left the room. I was then sorry that I had used the information that I had received from our security team that was watching over Lori in the Philippines. It had been hard for me to believe, but I had photos that came along with the report.

Lori stayed at the house that night, catching a flight out the next day. Except for the children, there were no goodbyes.

The next thing that would pop up was Jerry called with a story to tell. Seemed our boy Harry had changed his ways in prison. Harry had met a man friend at the movie. They came out of the theater together and found Harry's car not starting, and the man friend gave a ride to Harry in his car, leaving Harry's car there. The girls then had pulled in front of the man friend's car and slammed on the brakes. Both men got out and got sprayed with my mixture, causing both men almost immediately to pass out. The man friend was left in the driver's seat of his car. While Harry would take a ride that he wouldn't remember. Jerry said that Harry would arrive at the Nassau airport within three hours. I said that we'd have Lucy and the Authorities there waiting. It had taken some time, but justice for Lucy and Carla would now be complete.

I prepared and sent word to the Prince what had taken place with the attack on Pearl and Najima, to warn them from having any dealings with the Russians. To our big surprise, the Russians had already been there before Pearl was attacked. Not surprisingly, Maximus was there now doing test flights with Saudi pilots riding along. It seemed the Russians were upset that Maximus had beat them there. I wanted to but didn't ask how long Maximus had been there and where he was during the Sub attack. Since we didn't see anything but lights, we couldn't be sure it was Maximus nor what Vehicle was used. After all, we were talking about Pearl being attacked. Oh, how complicated this could get. Well, it was too late for the Saudi's to ask about whether they could trust Maximus. Asking me before the Saudi's put Maximus in the driver's seat would have put me in an uncomfortable position. I felt good not being in that position.

As things went, Lucy said she didn't recognize Harry. This I knew could jeopardize our case against him. The first three, Lucy had picked out of a lineup saying she would never forget any of their faces. We would need the Navy's assistance with their records, but even then, I didn't believe the Bahamian Government would put him on trial, much less convict him. The Bahamian court agreed to hold him and give us 30 days to produce some solid evidence. Lucy apologized over and over for not recognizing the man that had killed her friend. Jerry said he had gotten his man.

The Navy said they would not corroborate, this due to us having three of their men in jail with the Jag lawyers not getting access to Lucy. The only place I thought we might get help was from one of the three that were serving long terms in Bahamian cells.

Turned out that all three offered information on Harry. Each of the three wanted to sell Harry down the road for a reduced sentence.

We hadn't heard anything much from Lori; we did receive information from the Black Devils that were still there on guard. Malcolm sent me a letter saying how sorry he was how it had turned out. He wanted me to know that he would keep an eye on the children as they returned.

Najima spent a lot of time on the computer with her studies and TESS. June was June; she was more affectionate with me, gaining more confidence in Najima, who started treating June as a sister. We would see if that would stay in place as Najima would get her leg free today. Yes, that big nasty cast was coming off. Pearl was now in the U.K. at the facility building the new stile Harriers. Pearl was there to watch them build her newest model jet fighter. The U.S. military had ordered 6 of the new Harriers. Of course, my old friend Joe was still over there, now having two children with Deanna's Wendy Michelle. The Iron Lady had retired in 1990. Pearl got to meet with her telling me how much she liked her.

The Iron Lady had visited the factory and had seen the first Newly designed Harrier rolled out of the hanger. You guessed it; Pearl was the Test Pilot.

Gary had been upset with me when I took him and his sister back to General Santos. Since I delivered Gary back to General Santos, he had not spoken a single word to me.

It was now the last week of November; Najima and I were on the way to pick up the children when we received an urgent message from the Saudis requesting assistance. Our commercial flight was diverted to Hawaii, where we would be met there by Tommy, who would fly us to Riyadh. At the first notice of trouble, Dan and our number one C-130 would also head toward Riyadh.

CHAPTER XVIII

THE MISSING SAUDI VEHICLE

OUR WELCOMING PARTY AT THE Riyadh airport was missing the Prince; the reception didn't look or act friendly.

At the Palace, we were taken directly to the King. Najima was wearing her Muslim married Women's clothes and was welcomed by the King.

What Pearl and I had worried about was now a reality.

The King said that both the Vehicle and Maximus were missing. The King claimed that Maximus had stolen the Vehicle and he wanted it back. The King said that a price for the return of the Vehicle and Maximus's head was to be offered at once! You must have known, the King said, but you did not warn us. The guards were no match for the Vehicle, he said. The Vehicle escaped then helped with Maximus's departure. Najima's first words to the King were said in Arabic, My King she said, can you explain? The King stood and took Najima's hand and walked. We were first led to Maximus's quarters. As guards opened the room's doors, the King didn't have to point to the hole in the ceiling. The King said that they believed that the Vehicle had operated on its own and come for

Maximus. The King looked at me and again said we hadn't warned them that the Vehicle could work independently. I then asked if they were sure the Vehicle had freed Maximus? The King said that the Vehicle had released itself first and then come for Maximus. Can I see where the Vehicle was at the time of its escape? I asked the King? As we walked, Najima asked what I was thinking? I asked her if the Vehicle could have left on its own, why now, and why come back for Maximus? I asked the King if we could view any security videos that they might have. The King's head of security was also not available.

In speaking to the next in line with security, we heard a much different view of things. There were time laps that didn't show a video of either incident. The before and then after showed a video gap of over 24 hours. The King said that there was an electronic issue. The King looked tired and worried. He spoke to Najima in Arabic, stating that they might have lost the one thing that could keep his Kingdom safe. Point blank, I asked the King if he had seen the missing footage of the security tapes? The King said that we had seen the same that was shown to him. I told the King that if there were any chance of having the Vehicle returned, we'd have to find out what had taken place during the missing parts of the tapes. We would need the freedom to investigate and interview witnesses. The King asked if there was the possibility of getting the Vehicle back? The possible is done today I said. The impossible takes longer. In all this, the King had not let out anything that looked like a smile. The King said that we could ask anything of anyone and go anywhere; just get the vehicle back. The King said he would be retiring to his quarters.

My first security question was to see the Laser guns that we had left with the Prince. Not one, but both were missing. The next stop was to see the Prince. The Prince was in his quarters, but it looked like the king's guards were holding him. The Prince was glad to see us but happier to see Najima than me. The Prince apologized for not seeing her in the hospital but said he knew she was well cared for. The Prince asked to speak to Najima alone. I could tell he wasn't going to talk with me in the room. I asked if, while they talked, I could go to the rooftops of both buildings? The Prince in Arabic told the guards at the door to take me up on the roofs where the cuts had been made. Before exiting the Prince's quarters, I asked if Najima would be safe with him? The Prince said that Najima could not be harmed while in his presents.

I kissed Najima and was off to the rooftops.

The first roof was that of where the Vehicle had been stored. The building was made of poured concrete with mechanical steel doors. The fine cut roof hole seemed to be done with a laser; I was sure of it. However, the cut had been made from the outside, not the inside out. The cut was slanted so that the concrete roof would not fall in but could be lifted outward. I was sure the cut had been made from the outside and was larger than it should have been. The cuts were made unevenly, I thought, maybe by hand. In the almost center of the concrete roof slab that had been removed and replaced, there had been drilled or cut a hole in which the spot was used to place in some hooking device. To me, the roof as was the Vehicle had been lifted out; it must have taken the time and made lots of noise. I looked at the view from the top; there was no way someone hadn't seen and heard this operation. My thoughts were racing; I would have wagered that Maximus's roof would be the same but, it was not.

Najima joined me on the roof where Maximus seemed to have exited; the rooftop here also looked to have been cut using a laser. However, this cut was small and precisely cut with the cutout circle falling into the room's floor. Najima did not see the roof where the Vehicle had exited. Najima right away said that it looked as if the Vehicle had done as the King said and come for Maximus. I then wondered if Maximus had one of those golden wrist bracelets on;

the only time I had seen him, he had on that odd-looking jumpsuit that would have covered any bracelet.

Najima said that the Prince had told her that he had nothing to do with the Vehicle nor Maximus disappearing. The Prince also told Najima that he had nothing to do with mounting an attack on us when we stayed at the Oasis. He had at that time spoken with the King, and the King had agreed to them only having the one Vehicle here in Riyadh.

The Prince and the King were, however, disappointed that we had left without saying goodbye. The Prince said that the King placed him under guard for his safety as the King's brother had wanted to have him executed, blaming the Prince for the Vehicle's disappearance. The Prince had said he was sure that we would not again see their Security head. The Prince told Najima that we were not safe here and should leave before nightfall.

We asked to see the King on our way out and were told that the King was resting and not to be disturbed.

We would exit out the front Palace doors and then the gate. Dan was not at the gate waiting, and we were concerned about getting into one of Royal's transports or even a taxi. There was not many privet cars but Najima stopped one and we quickly got in. The car's driver was a merchant and quickly informed us that he could not act as a taxi. I pulled out a small roll of hundreds, and the car jerked forward. Our cell phones did not work, and I felt we were; no I knew we were being followed. Arriving at the airport, we thanked the driver and went through the airport doors. There were several guards at our gate. The Saudi guards seemed confused by what Najima told them. Whatever she said, she didn't stop talking, and they didn't stop listening.

Najima grabbed my arm and pushed toward the gate's open door. The guard's hesitation allowed us to get ahead and enter our plane and shut the cabin door behind us. The guards did knock on the doors, but our plane moved backward away from the gate. Tommy's cockpit door was left open, and I explained that we needed to get airborne at once.

With our Leer now moving toward the runway, our pilots were ordered to return to the gate. Our pilots said that we had a medical emergency aboard and we were headed to the runway and would not accept any interference. It wasn't another minute when the tower was buzzed by what we were sure was Pearl. Dan had requested Pearl's assistance as her Harrier was faster and closer than our C-130. Of course Pearl had now used her laser to limit the towers ability to view what was going on. When we hit the runway, the throttle was pushed forward for takeoff. Najima, now translating verbal instructions from Dan, warned the Saudis that the ground lasers were now in our control and, if necessary, would be used to assist our successful take off and exit. Our Leer was now in the air and rising.

Pearl speaking in Latin, told Najima that she was low on fuel and would not make it out of the kingdom's airspace. Najima and TESS translating simultaneously, Dan said that landing at the U.S. base was out of the question. We took a heading toward Qatar. Our leer had been fueled In Riyadh, Pearl said she was on fumes. We contacted the Qatar government and requested assistance. The Israel's were also contacted, the Israelis were in route to the sea side of Saudi's north eastern border. The Israelis were warned off by the Saudi's. Pearl would have to bail out just 150 miles from the sea. We saw her Harrier hit the ground hard, making a large fire ball. We circled around and got a visual of Pearl's parachute.

A very short time later, Pearl radioed that she was good.

Our best hopes were for the Israelis to come in with a copter and pick her up. It wouldn't be necessary, a written text appeared on the TESS screen. "Its Pearl, I have been rescued" then a pause then the screen said that she had been rescued by her "Uncle." "Meet you on the Hill," she wrote.

All of this had taken place so fast. We had now received Radio contact from the U.S. base here in Saudi, the communication said that they had sent in a rescue team for our downed pilot. TESS pointed out that two F16s were on the way, as well as three helicopters. The F16s were 2 minutes out, approaching fast. Dan made an open transmission that confirmed that our pilot was uninjured and did not require assistance. "We repeat, we are not in need of assistance". Our leer was now headed north-northeast toward the Persian Gulf. We sent a coded message to the Israelis that their rescue services would not be needed; however, our refueling requirements would stand as agreed.

Dan, now closing in fast was quick to warn off the passing two F16s, seemed they wanted a better look. The U.S. helicopters did not turn back, and TESS showed them circling the crash site, one landing long enough to retrieve Pearl's parachute. The F16s stayed with us until out of Saudi air space. Two of the U.S. copters then landed near the Harrier crash site. They might have been looking, thinking that maybe our pilot hadn't made it out.

One thing for sure is that we hadn't, so they hadn't picked up any other planes or copters on radar that could have picked Pearl up. If it was the Saudi Vehicle that picked up Pearl, and we had no doubt that it was, that would explain why no one had picked up the rescue on the radar.

We were refueled in air as agreed by the Israelis, it would be hours before we were home. We had sent messages that our Philippine trip had been canceled. I knew that our delay wouldn't go over good with Gary. He was already a bit upset with me. Lori would not know what had happened, and I wanted it kept that way.

Landing at Nassau, we were met by Pearl and June. Najima was the first one down the stairs. Pearl and Najima were the first hug. Mine with June was the next; then we joined the hug of Pearl's and

Najima's. I asked about Maximus; Pearl said he was gone. It seems Maximus's plan was as we thought. He had wanted the Vehicle and now had it. Does he know I asked? I don't think so, Pearl said; I didn't have the heart to tell him. And the first Vehicle I asked? He claimed he doesn't have it, Pearl said.

Pearl said that Maximus said it was the American's that attempted to take the Vehicle, the King's Brother was involved and had cleared the way. Maximus felt that if the King lost the Vehicle, his brother felt the King would be disgraced, and the brother would take over having the U.S. backing for the changeover. It was the bracelet Pearl said, TESS and the Vehicle broke free from it's captures and rescued Maximus as the First Vehicle had rescued us from the Russians. TESS, Pearl said, is just what Rodgers said it is, artificial intelligence; it thinks and acts on its own. Maximus said that the bracelets put out some signal when the holder is in personal danger.

All this brought my thought back to when I had gone to the movies and watched "The Terminator" in that movie; what was left of humans fighting Robots sent a Robot back in time to protect the human Rebel that had started the revolution against the Robots. The Robots were sending a Robot back in time to kill the leader as a boy, thus thinking the rebellion might not have even started. Thus far no robots but, we do have TESS, which is a computer that is programmed to protect whoever has these golden bracelets. I had only read two books that I could remember, "The Lion's Pawl" and "The Count of Monte Cristo," but I had seen movies that were made about books that Jules Verne had written. Jules Verne wrote stories that had flying Machines and Submarines long before there were such things. Then I wondered if maybe Jules Verne was born with four toes. Einstein had all that wild hair; maybe it was a wig hiding a big head.

Najima brought me back from my thoughts, saying we should be heading to General Santos to get the children. Najima was correct. Najima would stay put and care for the children while June and I would get Gary and Joe-Anne.

CHAPTER XIX

BACK TO GENERAL SANTOS

GARY AT ALMOST 5 YEARS old was big for his age. His golden hair was long and wavy with the biggest brown eyes you ever saw. Malcolm had the children at the airport when we arrived at General Santos. Malcolm told the story that Gary had snuck out of the house early that morning and was found walking to the airport. When Gary saw me, he came running, jumped up to my chest, and latched on; please, Papi, he said, please don't ever leave me here again. Joe-Anne was by then hugging my leg not letting go. I nestled down and picked her up also into my arms. With tears rolling down my cheeks I told them that I loved then and had missed them so much.

On the short trip to the house, we learned that Malcolm and Mia were expecting their second child at any moment. How the time was flying by. Malcolm said it was to be a boy with the name of James. Malcolm also said that things on the port were not going well. The port workers were on a slow down, this was costing delays such that we now had our ship anchored in the bay. The fruit company that owned the dock had declared an emergency and Lori's ship and cargo were being put on hold. Everything was out of wack. Our generators, Malcolm said were wearing out and breaking down. The situation, Malcolm said, was critical.

Once at the Santos House I changed clothes and would head to the port with Malcolm. The town had changed, the streets were paved, and there was new construction everywhere.

Before arriving to the port we hit the traffic, the truck lines into the port were long. Malcolm noted that the fruit that arrived in small trucks, waiting to get into cold storage would suffer quality or could even be rejected. The ride that should have taken ten minutes took us forty.

The inside of the port was more chaos; there were trucks and containers everywhere. When we found Lori I couldn't believe my eyes. Lori looked sickly; she had lost maybe 20 pounds or more. I let out the loudest whistle I could. Lori heard the whistle, dropped what she had in her hands, and came running. Lori stopped just 3 feet from me and looked at me. I'm a little girl of 21 years old, she said. I've made some terrible mistakes; I know you will not take me back, but I am in big trouble in my life and here on the port. Right now, she said, more than anything, I need a hug and, if possible, one of those for real kisses. I made a large step forward as did she. It was the hug and kiss that she said she needed. When the kiss stopped, and I had her in my arms, I could feel her skinny, frail body next to mine. Where is Nilo I asked? Lori said that Nilo was aboard with the reefer technicians trying to save two shrimp loads. What's the present temperature of the shrimp? I asked? Lori said minus 3 degrees Fahrenheit. Both I asked? I believe so, she said. Any other problems aboard I asked? The people she answered, they don't seem to care about the cargo. The fruit companies people too, I asked? Lori said it had started with their people having what they called a welga which. I then broke in, saying the words, work strike. I asked Lori how many electric plugs she had available; she looked at me and said containers were waiting for electricity. The fruit company, any of their cargo without electricity, I asked? Lori said that she had given the fruit company the priority and believed that all the fruit company's cargo was connected. Maybe not without problems but connected. I told Malcolm to go and fetch Nilo, then Nilo's son.

When Nilo arrived I asked him about the shrimp loads and their temperatures? With his answers, I told him to bring them down from the ship and send them back to the cold storage, making sure that the containers were connected to an underslung generator during the ride. Nilo looking ashamed, said that most of the chassis generators were not working. Malcolm was now back with Nilo's son. I asked Malcolm about the freezers? Malcolm said we were in good shape with a steady temperature of minus 18 degrees or lower. And space, I asked? We are good Malcolm said. Ok, I said, I told Nilo to take the shrimp loads down and send the cargo to the freezers. Then I said to stop processing our cut fruit except what's going to the fruit company. I then asked Nilo what the workers wanted? Nilo's reply was short, "more money." All the costs have been going up and up, Nilo said. I looked at Lori and asked if, before the labor troubles if the bottom line was good? Lori said she thought so because the cash flow had always been good. How much of a raise are they asking for, I asked? Nilo said that our people would be happy with 20% but that our people already made more than the fruit company's workers and that the tuna factory's people even made less. Looking at Nilo, I asked where Ninong was on all this? Nilo said that Ninong was in support of the work slow down. I asked Malcolm to take Lori home and asked Nilo to set up a meeting with Ninong. I asked Nilo's son if our computer in the port's office was still in use? The answer was yes, and I signaled him to lead the way.

The fruit company's manager was in the office. We hadn't met; he could tell I wasn't a happy puppy. I looked him in the eyes and told him that if I found that his workers and the tuna factory workers were being underpaid that I would personally hold him responsible. I then gave him the chance to complain about Lori and the services that she was supplying. Mr. Howard said that they knew she was having a hard time but knew that she had grown too fast. He said that the slowdown didn't allow Lori's ship, space at the port. We understand that the crane is hers but the crane contract as well as the cold storage and electric contracts all state that we shall have the priority of their use. I asked about plans for another birth? Mr. Howard said that yes, they had such a plan but that their needs wouldn't start construction until 1994 or 1995. I asked the cost? Mr. Howard said $30,000,0000 and rising.

I could see what was going on; the fruit company was pushing Lori out.

As I walked out of the port office, they're standing at the steps was Ninong. Hello old friend, I said as I walked down the steps. At the steps bottom, he was waiting for a big hug. Ninong patted my back and said that he thought I would have shown up before now. Ninong said that even Gary said he thought you had forgotten him and his sister. I looked at him and asked, how can we make this right? The people only want what is fair, Ninong said. Inflation is up over 50%, in January the fruit company gave raises of 8%. Nino said the workers can afford rice, beans and fish, but they see the city making big improvements, motorbikes, and even cars. Most port and factory workers still Live in grass huts without bathrooms or running water. Lori is a strong woman but she needs a strong man. The young man from the shipping company came a-courting, oh yes Ninong said. Flew in on his privet plane. I understand he asked her to marry him, but she turned him down. Of course, Nino said, young Brian didn't find the woman he had last seen. I got that bit of information too from Gary, Ninong said. Gary is a boy that reminds me of someone I used to know, Ninong said. Joe-Anne looks like her mom. Both children, Ninong said, are doing without a father or a mother.

Ok, I said, Nilo, keep the banana cutting going, but only load what the fruit company wants, use our 30 slot guarantee for all the shrimp you can pack, then beef with any extra space we have. Nilo corrected me, saying that we had 45 slots on each of the Crowlbe ships. Ok I said, fill those slots but nothing more. Nilo asked what to do with the extra bananas that got cut. I said to give away what could be used for live stock then if necessary burn the rest. Should we stop the planting of the new acreage, Nilo asked? No, I said.

We then all three entered Nino's truck. We drove to the end of the peer. No, Nilo said there's no room for even a small ship to berth. A roll roll could come in at it's stern I said. All we need is to drive in enough piling to hold her in place, I said. Nilo asked if I thought the fruit company would give permission for the operation? They'll give permission, I said. I looked at Ninong and asked if the fruit company had purchased the land for their proposed new port? Ninong said no but that he knew where it was and how much it was going to cost. Can we buy it today I asked? I'm the Governor Ninong declared.

We passed by the property then I asked Nilo and Ninong to make the arrangements for the purchase. They would drop me off at the Santos house, where I would arrange the money we needed.

At the house, I found that June was upstairs with Lori. When June heard my call, she came down the stairs and said we needed to get Lori to a Doctor in Manila. I went upstairs and told Lori that she was going to that first doctor that we had seen. I would send word to Tommy, and he would transport Lori and June to Manila at once. I did not tell Lori of my plans but did tell her not to worry; it wouldn't take long to turn this all around. Lori looked at me and asked, all of it? We shall see, I said.

I then went into the office and shut the door. Before I could even start typing my log in there was a knock on the door. I opened the door and there stood Gary and Joe-Anne. Can we watch you work, Gary asked? Sure, I said come on in. I looked at them and said that they mustn't talk about what they hear. I told them that loose lips sink ships, and we wouldn't want to sink mommy's ship, would we? No sir they both said.

I then sent a message that I wanted Evette on the next commercial flight and Lourdes to send me $10,000,000. I wanted a message sent to Robin that I wanted to lease two vessels like the Striders that we had previously used. If Robin didn't have in his fleet, I wanted him to find them for me. I was going to come into the dock from the stern. I would also need two small tugboats. Robin didn't live in Miami; he was now living in New York with the title of President of the largest Marine Leasing Company globally. If he couldn't get something done in the Marine Business, well, it just couldn't be done.

Generators, I told Lourdes that I wanted 10 Cat generators of 500 KW all set up with 460-volt reefer plugs. I wanted spares for all. I would also need 5,000 feet of 460-volt cable and male and female reefer plugs to make extensions, 500 or so. Malcolm was now there at my office door, reminding me that we needed a lot of nitrogen and fittings.

Tommy had gotten the word, and the car was here, ready to take Lori and June to the airport. Both stopped by for a hug and kiss then they were off.

The children didn't let my legs go; they followed me around the house until their bedtime.

It was after 10 p.m. when Ninong stopped by the house; Ninong brought with him good news; he said that the property would cost $3,000,000. The owners, he said, were a group of the town's businessmen, including himself. They had negotiated with the fruit company, and the fruit company had signed a letter of intent. Ninong and his group wanted to be partners with the fruit company, but the fruit company had refused. Nino then said that they still wanted a share of the port. I said $2,000,000 plus 10 percent. Nino said $2,500,000 and 20 percent. I then said I'd pay the total price and share 10 percent. Nino stuck out his hand. I then went to the computer and sent a message to Lourdes to get Matt here ASAP with our two engineers from Paix. I then sent a message to Jerry, "will need two of your birds to shuttle supplies to General Santos." His two C-130 from the war had now been returned and we're again without TESS. "If you need more equipment, contact Jack, he will assist"

It looked like we were on our way to building a port. Ninong then looked at me and asked about the people? I looked at him and said that I was not in agreement with any work slow down. I told him that if he and his business people would put up $500,000 of their land money that I would match it. $1,000,000 to make any reasonable no-interest loans to whoever worked on the farms or port operations from either company. There will be no negotiated pay raise on Lori's group until after the people start giving 100 % to the company. The fruit company, I said, will see the writing on the wall, and I believe once their people also start giving 100%, we will negotiate a good raise. Ninong said that the matching of my loan money would be met. He would call a separate meeting of all farm and port workers and give them his recommendation; then, they could decide what to do.

The following day June called and said that the doctor would admit Lori into a private hospital. June said that Lori would most likely be there for a few days and then stay away from work for another two weeks. June suggested that Lori go back with us to Nassau. I thought it was good that Lori goes to Nassau, but I would need to stay put for a while.

I had sent a hand written letter to the Saudi King. The Prince was released and was looking to come to visit. The purpose of the visit was to make a reward offer for the missing Vehicle and, of course, thank us for at least stopping the King from being overthrown. The Prince joked with Najima, whom he had spoken to, that the King was sending another gift like the first one. Of course the Prince was referring to Najima. Najima did not think it funny.

I now sent a message to Pearl that I needed her to stay out of trouble for at least until I got back. Pearl said that she wanted to spend time with her mother Lori. Najima said the children and her were doing fine. Najima said that she missed me terribly and now more than ever wanted a child of her own.

The big news was that Johnny and Caroline were only waiting for my return to get married. It seemed that I was again going to be a grandfather.

The next day I few to Manila to visit Lori. Lori was in a privet room receiving fluids intravenously. June left the room saying she would go shopping for gifts for the children. June said she would return the following day as there were lots of children to buy for. I was sure June would do that shopping she was talking about but thought it was her way of giving Lori and me some time alone.

Lori and I talked a lot, I told her my plans with the two roll-on ships and of all the purchases I had made. We will build our port, I declared; we will call ports that Brian's Grand Father doesn't; at least that's the plan I said. Your ship will be idle for quite some time; when you're up to it, call Brian and ask if they could use the vessel in any of their services for about a year. Better yet, on the way to Nassau, you can stop by their office on your way home. Lori then told me that Brian had come and asked her to marry him. I could see it in his eyes Lori said, he was surprised at my looks. I might have said yes she said, but it wasn't the time. He'll be back I said, in a few weeks you'll be as good as new. By the time you visit Brian's office, the fruit company will have contacted them to consult on what should be their next step. I'm sure that the Fruit company won't approve of them leasing your idle ship. Lori said she would do as I wished.

I spent the night and left when June showed up. Once the few days in the hospital were up, Lori and June would fly back to General Santos, then fly back to Manila, then directly from Manila to San Francisco. Then on to Nassau.

My next few weeks went by in a blink of an eye. Evette had shown up and would be in charge of all the money spent, plus inbound equipment and parts. The land purchase was made before the fruit company even knew about it. My engineer group was here on the ground; Matt had hired and brought an engineer whose specialty was building ports.

As Lori and June had arrived in Nassau, Tommy took Najima to Lake Charles, where she caught one of the supply planes heading this way. Najima had now been here a week. Gary didn't take to her right away, but Joe-Anne followed Najima everywhere. Najima said that Joe-Anne didn't stop asking questions.

Funny how things turned out, Ninong and several of the old rebels were Muslims, as was Najima. In front of Najima, Ninong asked me, how many wives you got? Najima answered, he doesn't know. She and Ninong laughed.

It had only been three weeks since I arrived in General Santos, today we were driving the pilings that would hold our inbound leased ships, the first coming in two days. Aboard the first ro-ro ship were two new Ottawa mule trucks along with ten new chassis combos and two new 45-ton reach stackers.

Since Nino's meeting with our workers, from that moment, their attitudes changed. The fruit company had asked that I fly to Costa Rica for a meeting. I would not accept until I had loaded out our first ship.

Najima and I had been sleeping in the Santos master bedroom which of course was Lori's. Guess who showed up today? Yes it was Lori. Still thin but looking much better.

When Lori arrived at the Santos House, Najima was in the pool with Gary and Joe-Anne. After greeting the children, Lori headed up to her room. Lori then came down and asked Najima to move her things to one of the guess rooms. Najima moved both hers and my clothes. Lori didn't wait for me to come home; she changed clothes and headed to the port. Not much on the old port had changed. I say old port as there were now lots of equipment working on the property a bit to the east. Yes, this was the new port. When Lori reached me, I was ankle-deep in mud, yes this was General Santos, and it had been raining the last couple of days. None the less I heard Lori's whistle and then saw her making her way to me. When she got within that two-foot mark from me, she stopped. I want to come back to you she said; I will do anything you wish. We can walk away from all this at this moment and not look back, she said. Please take me back she asked? For real I asked? Yes she said. You'll come back without conditions, I ask? Lori said yes. I then made that last step and got that hug and kiss.

Lori's first question was where all the fill was coming from? Well, I said, we had to buy ten new dump trucks along with several pieces of equipment. We purchased a bit of high land and are moving that material almost 15 miles to here. How long will it take to complete Lori asked? I looked at her and said about a year.

Lori said that she would return to the house and make friends with Najima, but that tomorrow she would be here right next to me working. I looked at her and said that she was limited to 8 hours a day, 5 days a week. Got it I asked? Yes, sir, Lori replied.

Lori then went back to the house and moved her things to the guest room, and told Najima she was to move her and my things back to the master.

Another week went by and we now had one sailing of the first leased ro-ro ship under our belt. The ship of course didn't go out full, and I hadn't ordered to restart up with our fruit cargo until we knew for sure that all of this was working. Lori had contacted her clients and assured them that she was back on track, inviting them all to come to General Santos to see the progress she was making on her new port. As the new generators arrived, we sent the older stuff to the states to rebuild or sell. What generators that were reworked would be sent back and used for spares.

Things were going good, at the house things were going better than I could imagine. I was getting the best of two worlds. I was now getting two hot showers a day.

I was confident that our ships would soon be going out full and that our engineers, along with Matt's assistance, would complete our new port on schedule. It was time to go visit the fruit company in Costa Rica. Costa Rica of course was Evette's old stomping ground, but she was needed here. Mr. Shoemaker was no longer with the fruit company; he was replaced with a man that I didn't know. When I called, I suggested that all parties that were involved be at this meeting. The meeting was set; we had ten days to get ready.

I had started the cutting and loading of our bananas and pineapple, we would not use our slots on Brian's ship this trip, Brian's ship would still go out full due to them not using Lori's container ship that was still anchored in the bay. Our second ro-ro ship would have been sailing with about 20 containers short of full, however at the last moment Lori picked up a customer that would also buy canned tuna. The tuna factory was backed up with shipments due to the shortage of ship cargo space. Mr. Mitchocomi's group was happy to add their cargo to fill our ship. Yes, our second ro-ro ship would go out full.

Once our ship had departed Lori and Najima would visit Manila so that Lori could make her last Doctor's appointment. The girls left early that morning and would return that same afternoon.

That night I got the news, Lori was pregnant with our third child and Najima said that we would have a four toe. Yes both girls were pregnant and due within a week of each other. Both girls were all smiles; they asked if this made me happy? I knew that Najima was in the hunt for a child but wasn't counting on Lori having another. Speaking of counting, I would now have nine children. I hugged the girls, telling them both that I was ecstatic over the news.

Now we had a new problem, the girls said they had nothing to wear. Najima had really not been shopping, and Lori, well, looked better, but only being weeks pregnant, she still was shy about ten pounds. The girls said they wanted to meet June in Miami and go shopping. It was arranged, and we all, including Gary and Joe-Anne, would head to Miami.

With the news of us being so close to Nassau, Johnny called and asked if we could stop in at Nassau long enough for Caroline and him to get married, another dress for the girls.

June had brought with her some help to watch the children while we shopped. It was Burdines first, then Jordon Marsh. June, at 41 years old, looked fantastic; she looked 30, Lori at 21 with her weight loss, looked no more than 18, and no one would believe she had two children and another on the way. Najima at 20 looked like 25 or so. Najima reminded me of Salinas so much I hadn't seen it until this very day. All of the girls were beautiful beyond belief. Us shopping together made me think of a TV show that I had once seen named Charlie's Angles. My girls would pick out a dress; then the other two would go into the dressing room and help put it on, then come out and model it for me. By the time we finished, it was three days later, and there were bags everywhere. Of course, Lori brought closes for her two, and June got for the rest of the children.

We arrived in Nassau, and the airport was full of friends and family and, of course, security. The children had all changed so much. The biggest changes were Sunshine and Pearl. Sunshine, now almost 48 years old, was standing straight, had thinned out, and looked as bright as she is. Pearl now 25 was the leader of the gang. She looked like she was the cat that had the mouse in her mouth, just waiting to burst out like she had something to tell me. Having Rodgers at the airport to greet us most likely had something to do with what Pearl was holding to tell me. Pearl's hugs were mostly for Lori and Najima, but I got some of that too. The children were happy to see me, but Gary and Joe-Anne got most of their attention.

The small wedding would take place at the Hill Top House; neither Johnny nor Caroline were much of churchgoers.

Lourdes had flown in with Dan and Shirley from Paxi, Jack and Cindy were there, as were Charles and Madilyn. What was to be a small group was not so small at all. Caroline made a beautiful bride. Johnny and Caroline had chosen Eleuthera to build their house on the water not too far from Charles, Madilyn, Jack, and Cindy. Eleuthera had many good points as Nassau, and Paradise Island was becoming too doggone busy. Johnny as well as Charles and Jack had their own planes at the small airport on Eleuthera.

Caroline had also learned to fly. I was proud of them both for their achievements and for Caroline to enjoy flying after almost not surviving a horrific air crash. Neither of the two had living parents. The wedding reminded me a bit of my surprise wedding to Salinas. I watched carefully that there were no such plans for me here as It would have been me marrying both and June and Najima.

During the wedding, I noticed something with a cover on it parked on Pearl's Harrier's landing pad. Pearl was close by, and I asked her what was under the cover? Pearl said that once the newlyweds had gone, she and Rodgers would take off the cover.

CHAPTER XX

THE NEW BREED OF VEHICLE

I T WAS ALMOST 2 AM, and I was getting sleepy; Caroline and Johnny, along with most guests, had gone when Pearl led me by the hand to the spot; using her other hand, she pulled off the cover.

I didn't have to ask what it was; it was either one of the Vehicles or a replica. Pearl now dropped my hand and walked to the ship. She opened wide her left hand and placed it on the side of the ship. As she did, a small door opened, and Pearl stepped back. The outside was the same, but the inside was much different. This ship didn't have a water chamber. The space still cramped was used for more battery power; it was powered by two electric engines that could recharge the batteries in flight or underwater. This ship's controller was in a sealed container that once the seal was broken or removed from the ship, it would meltdown. I stepped in and, of course, bumped my head. This was a two Pilot ship with one bunk. Once inside, Pearl stepped in and closed the door behind her. She sat at the controls and said for me to sit tight. The ship lifted and we were off into the air. Pearl had motioned me to put on my helmet, when doing so a familiar voice greeted me. Good morning Commander the voice said, it of course was the voice of TESS. We were air born traveling west at a speed of 600 mph. It felt as if we were not moving at all, I asked where we were going and Pearl said she had another surprise. I was looking at several screens, one that had a panoramic view of our surroundings. I could see we were flying toward the Island of Andros getting very close, fast. All of a sudden, the ship dove into the channel. I could hardly tell we were below the surface but I knew we were. Our speed hitting the water had slowed down to 50 mph then once underwater we were moving at a much slower speed. It had to be pitch dark down here but the screen hadn't changed. Pearl said I was to blow out my ears as if I were diving. The screen showed we were at a depth of 300 feet when I noticed what looked like a hole in the side of the western edge of the channel. As we approached the hole, I knew we were headed inside. As we entered the hole, the screen changed, showing only the cave's entrance behind us and what was in front of us. We went in about 3000 feet then turned upward until we left the water with the screen now showing a large air pocket. Pearl then put the ship down on a platform and while still in the ship, tested the outside oxygen levels. The the door opened, and Pearl took off her helmet, then Pearl stepped out. Of course, I followed, after again bumping my head, once out of the ship, there it was. I started to ask but, Pearl answered before I got it out of my mouth. Yes, she said, it's my Grand Father's Ship. I don't know why but I wasn't surprised. Victoria had said that the Vehicle would find Pearl when the time was right. Although it should have been dark in here, it seemed almost daylight; this cave was not man-made, nor was its entrance. Pearl said that if that 1945 salt bomb that was dropped hadn't caught her Grand Father off guard, he could have been here where he would have survived. It was the Indian Chief that led my Grand Father down here, Pearl said. There are hand-made steps that once led to the surface. The land entrance has long been blocked from above and a door placed here at the bottom. Here in this cave, we found many secrets of my ancestors, Pearl said. I do not believe that my mother or for that matter my uncle, has ever been here. We I asked? Yes Pearl said, Sunshine and I.

We, yourself, Sunshine, and myself are the only ones living that know about this place.

The Saudi's Pearl said, will be in Nassau to meet with you to offer to buy the ship that came from the desert. I thought it a good idea to sell or even give them the ship we came here in. Them having the ship we built will restore the confidence in the King and Prince. Come Pearl said the surprises are not yet over. As Pearl walked around the corner more lighting appeared as did a large door that seemed to open on its own power. This room housed another Vehicle. It was a small machine that I was sure was used to make the original cave wide enough for her Grand Father's Vehicle to enter. My first thought was that if Pearl's Grand Father had this cave, why build another? Pearl again reading my mind said that the original cave was dug before the Indian Chief led her Grand Father to this cave. Her Grand Father made the room we were standing in as a warehouse and a shop where he stored and built things. This room is dried by a humidifier she said. Here there was also a computer station with some kind of rod that was drilled to just below the surface. The rod Pearl said allows communications. The last surprise is the treasure that our people have saved during our time here on earth. It must have taken many trips by my Grand Father to get it all here. There were boxes and boxes of it stacked one on top of the other.

I then glanced at my watch and said that the sun's rise would be starting soon and that we should be going not to be seen.

On our short trip back Pearl showed me that her new flying ship also had a bite to it. There were several lasers that could only be out gunned by the original Vehicles. The Prince, Pearl said, would be more than happy.

Pearl was right, the Prince and his group were redirected to Paxi. Pearl dropped me off at Hill Top and headed south. Pearl would be ready for the Prince when he arrived.

Me I though I would be taking a lonely cold shower but it didn't work out that way. Najima had sort of waited up for my return.

Tommy would be taking Najima and myself to Paxi to meet with the Prince. It was the Prince's first trip to Paxi. A military base on foreign ground the Prince said. Meeting the Prince from his plane, we went right where we had his surprise, there parked in a hanger, were two Vehicles parked side by side. The Prince looked in a amazement, you have recovered our ship he said! No Prince, I said we had built somewhat of a duplicate. Which is which, the Prince asked? Pearl walked to the new model and placed her hand on the ship, and the door opened. Would you like a ride Pearl asked? Is it safe the Prince ask? Safe, Pearl said if you're not on the other side of its lasers. The Prince started up, and I said to watch his head, but it was too late. The Prince turned and looked at me and said Pearl should have given him the helmet before climbing in. With Pearl in, the door was close behind them and we stepped back. The ship then lifted up and slowly moved out of the hanger on it's own power. The ship was gone for 30 minutes when it returned. When the Prince stepped out, he was white. He had one hand holding his head and the other over his heart. As his feet touched the ground, he said that they would like to purchase ten such ships. I looked at the Prince and said that this ship belongs to his Kingdom. The Prince then came to me and hugged me. The King, the Prince said, will be most pleased. Our tour ended at the Chateau, where of course, the Prince would notice Salinas's portrait. As all that would come into the Chateau for the first time, the Prince couldn't help but stop and stare. Najima mentioned that Salinas was the mother of three of our children. Najima, holding her stomach, then said, with mine we would have nine. The Prince noted all those wives and only nine children? Najima, the Prince said, should give you at least another three to make it an even dozen.

And Pearl the Prince asked, you have not chosen a husband? Then another surprise, Pearl then said she would marry an Israeli Pilot. I asked, does he know yet? Pearl laughed and said, no, but he soon will.

From the living room we passed into the study. The Prince asked what we had heard of their original ship? I said that other than Maximus picking up Pearl in the desert, we hadn't had any further contact with Maximus or their ship. The problem with searching for your ship is what we could do if we found it. I said that in a fight, at least one ship could be lost and maybe both. The risk I said is to high. I then waited and said that others would not stop from wanting what you have. We have, I said, programmed your new ship so that it can not be stolen unless your pilots steal it, but that even then, there was a built-in system that could override the pilots.

Pearl, you will train our pilots the Prince asked? Yes Pearl said, I will train them here at Paxi. How long will this take the Prince asked? Pearl said she wasn't sure how to answer that question? Maybe a year maybe two, she said, there is no room for errors she said, these ships are not built for crashing. You crash, you die she said; there's no bailing out. Yes, of course, the Prince said; he understood. I looked at the Prince and asked if we were good? The Prince stood and said yes.

At the airport, standing at Tommy's Leer, was Sunshine. As I approached, she opened up her arms, I was embraced, and Sunshine said she didn't remember if she ever thanked me for coming for her. I love my life, Sunshine said, and my family. Thank you she said. I told her that she had transformed into a beautiful butterfly. That she should only think in the future. You deserve to be happy, I said, and that it was I that thanked her for coming to us.

From Paxi, it was back to Hill Top to pick up Lori and head on over to Costa Rica for our big meeting. Our meeting in Costa Rica was no less important than the one with the Prince. The only difference was that we would be dealing with people that I believed had in mine to put us out of business.

We arrived in San Jose and checked into the hotel, the next morning at 9:00 a.m. sharp we were at the fruit companies headquarters. I of course was dress in one of my black suits while Lori and Najima were dress to kill. Brian was waiting in the lobby to meet us. Brian had not met Najima but, of course, just six months ago, had asked Lori to marry him. One could tell that he was happy to see Lori looking so good. Lori introduced Najima to Brian as a new member our family. I asked Brian if his Grand Father was here? Brian said that his Grand Father sent his apologies but that he would be representing the line. We were escorted to the President's office and were taken straight in. Young Mr. Mitchocomi was already in the office, Mr. Pierce, the new President of the fruit company, was seated behind his desk; he stood and held out his hand. Everyone was introduced, and there was some talk of how the families were.

Then Mr. Pierce spoke; Ms. Lori has put us in a labor predicament that has cost us all money and lost time. She overpays her workers, and it caused our workers to want the same and now even more.

I then broke in and said that Lori doesn't consider them her workers; she sees them as they are, her people. She has paid until now what was considered a fair wage. Your workers, including the Tuna Factory, especially the Tuna Factory, are underpaid, which has cost you. Then Mr. Pierce lashed out, saying that once again, I had taken something that was going to be theirs. My reply was that they didn't buy the port property because they didn't need it as yet, you blocked my wife's ship, and she had no choice but to move forward. Now, I said, you invited us here to voice your complaints or you have something in mind, I asked? I then looked at Brian and asked if they were backing out of our agreement for space? Brian said, no sir, our agreement stands. I then looked at Mr. Mitchocomi and asked if he wanted to sell me the Tuna Business? Mr. Mitchocomi said that his family was happy with the business. Looking at Mr. Mitchocomi, I asked, can you raise your people's pay by 50%? Mr. Mitchocomi said we will raise their pay by 30%. He then said that the Tuna Factory was not having the same problems as the port. The workers see that there are lines every day with people looking for jobs. I looked over at Lori, and she nodded her head yes. How are your expansion plans coming along I asked Mr. Mitchocomi? Mr. Mitchocomi looked at Mr. Pierce and said that they were told that Ms. Lori's Business would soon fold, and that the property was in a trust that also had your name on it for your children. But you still paid the lease I said. Yes Mr. Mitchocomi said we paid because we thought where was that possibility of things working in our favor. The price is good for you I asked? Yes Mr. Mitchocomi answered. Good enough that if I too sign the lease that you could raise your people's pay another 20% I asked? 10 % Mr. Mitchocomi answered, a total of 40% if you would sign. I then stood and put out my hand to Mr. Mitchocomi. Mr. Mitchocomi did the same.

I then looked back at Mr. Pierce and said that Lori was not going away. I then suggested that Lori take over the fruit companies on port restaurant, there Lori providing an excellent complimentary breakfast and lunch to all port workers of both companies. Next, I suggested that the fruit company raise the pay of their people by 20% and that Lori stay at the present pay rate. Mr. Pierce then said that we were using 20% of their dock without paying anything to them. I looked at Mr. Pierce and asked if he was going to assume Lori's cost for her ship setting in the harbor and the two ro-ro ships she leased? Mr. Pierce then said that the crane charges that were to go into effect on January one were too high. I said that's easy to fix; buy the crane. I looked at Lori and asked, there's a buy out clause in the contract, correct? Lori said yes. I looked at Mr. Pierce and said, then it's settled; on January one, you will buy the crane or pay the new rate. Mr. Pierce then looked at me and said he had not agreed to our suggestions but would study our proposal and get back to us within the next month. I said that would be fine but that a good source told me that his people were meeting tomorrow to decide whether to go on a full strike. Your strike will not affect our people, I said; if Lori can't provide her people with free meals, she will be forced to raise their pay another 10%. This possible raise will go into effect if your people decide go on strike. Once Lori raises her people that 10%, there will be no going back, I said. This is back mail! Mr. Pierce said. No, Sir I said, we have nothing to gain by you doing what's right. Black mail is a one sided deal; I'm sure your board will agree with our suggestions. I then stood and thanked Brian and Mr. Mitchocomi for their attendance.

Brian followed us out; Brian looked at me and said that his Grand Father said that I would be fair but stern. Brian then looked at Lori and said he was happy that things had worked out for her. Brian then looked at Najima and said, I don't guess your are single. Najima not looking at Brian, but looking straight at me said, no I'm happily married. Brian said some men have all the luck.

Mr. Pierce would call the hotel and confirm that Lori was to take over their port restaurant and they would immediately raise their port workers pay by 20%. What was left open was whether the fruit company would in January pay the new crane rate or buy the crane.

That same night Ninong and Nilo were both informed of our new agreement with the Fruit Company.

Nilo would become Lori's new business manager, while Malcolm would become second in charge. Nilo's wife would manage the port restaurant.

Pearl now had two Saudi pilots located at Paxi and would begin flight school with the Saudi ship we had offered them. A second ship was in production with the thought of it going to the Brits. Although the Iron Lady was no longer in power, I still held her and the Brits high in my thoughts. We were now in production of seven stealth-like Harriers in England. These jets were being built for the U.S. These jets were ordered before Pearl completing the first trial Vehicle, given to the Saudis. The U.S. would soon hear of our breakthrough and would be calling for a visit. The cost of building such a ship was just under $75,000,000, this due to all of the electronics and onboard computers. Parts and conductors being made of gold and other high cost materials. Rodgers working without a day off was still improving on materials becoming lighter, stronger, and our computers also smarter.

Pearl, Sunshine and myself would revisit the the newly found cave. We would use the our desert Vehicle as we would plan to be carrying out a maximum of 200 lbs of gold each trip. At that rate, it would take 15 trips to pay for the building of one new ship.

Today's trip to the cave we were delivering, the original controller that I switched. We now had three original controllers. I took the spare from the first cave, the one in the desert ship, and the one that I had switched with the other desert ship before we delivered it to the Saudis. We would now place the controller from the Saudi's desert ship into the ship in the new cave that was Pearl's Grand Father's ship. We now had two ships that were fully powered.

The time flew by very quickly, before I knew it both Lori and Najima were having babies, both boys. Najima's boy would be named Amir and Lori's Andrew. I now had nine biological children.

Within two months the New General Santos Port would be up and ready. The two new container cranes were already placed, with the travel railing needing their finishing touches. Lori's two ro-ro ships had been going out full for the past six months this with Lori still fulfilling her space quota with Brian's ships. Things couldn't have looked better; Nilo's wife had taken over the restaurant on the port, all port workers were getting two free meals a day, and Lori's group financials were right where they should have been.

My friend the U.S. President that only served one term was replaced by a Democrat. I now know no one in the Government sector. The new guys on the block don't know me either.

Pearl was still giving flight lessons to the two Saudi's but now she had 4 other students, two Brits and two Israelis. You might have guessed, one of the two Israelis was that Pilot that Pearl had taken a shine to.

The seven special Harriers had been delivered to the USAF but by now the U.S. had come up with some stealth design of their own. The U.S. Was in the process of building a stealth bomber that would house a TESS unit. Pearl and Rodgers were working on their number four Vehicle. None of the four dropped bombs nor shot any thrust-powered weapons. All were equipped with laser technology. Their latest model was being built as a twin of our two original Vehicles, water doors and all. We still were relying on batteries as our electrical power for these Vehicles. Rodger stated that the nuclear power rods were still years away.

Since Pearl's desert rescue and return to Hill Top, we had not heard from Maximus. Long before now, Maximus must have discovered that the controller in his Saudi Vehicle had been changed out. Maybe Maximus had made the necessary adjustments, and he had flown off into space. That, at least, was what I hoped had happened.

Melody and Sam we're now living with us in Nassau full time, Chubby had passed away from a heart attack, and Lilly had moved back to Miami to live with a younger sister whom she had helped bring in from Cuba. We had 9 children at the house. I had finally moved Lori's sailboat from Miami and docked it at Valentine's on Harbor Island. It was the first time since I was about eight years old that I had no active connection with the Coconut Grove Sailing Club.

All but my two youngest would go out sailing, fishing and diving with me almost on a daily bases.

We'd still dive and fish those same two sights that Johnny took me too on my first Bahama trip. Each trip we'd take to the eastern reefs or the first ship's wreck site, we'd carry with us two reefs of flowers. At those two sites, I would tell the children stories of my first trip to the Bahamas with my friend Rusty and how we met Angee's 13-year-old son, Johnny. Johnny, of course, was the boy that had guided me to the original treasure site. I would tell them about that first cannon sighting and how it started my drive to get back to the Bahamas. I would tell them of Michelle, but words couldn't describe how she looked wearing that short sleeve wet suit.

I often visit the graves of my wife Salinas and my first love, Deanna. Reefs, too, are dropped at the end of the Nassau Marina Dock, one for Cat and one for Willy. I haven't visited Joe-Anne's gravesite in years, but all the older children know of her and her story of bravery and sacrifice.

Angee and Betty are the only ones left that could tell a real story of my first Bahamian days. Yes Jena could tell some stories too if she was around. I had met Jena at my 21st birthday party that ended up where Benny attempted to bring me into the mob, it was there that same night I had my run-in with Giovanni. Benny told his group of men that I was now a Wise Guy, having made my first kill. When I told Benny and the group that I hadn't killed anyone, they all laughed. Jena was at the Club Royal when I confronted part of the group of seven on whom I believed had Michelle murdered. At that meeting Jena dressed and played the part of a Voodoo Queen. Jena scared the pants off Baby Doc. That night we ended up in a gun battle, us against the Haitian Navy.

It was Carson and I that stopped the would be kidnapers that were after Jena. Both Jena and Carson were on the trip where we flew into Port-a-Prince when Baby Doc and the Palace were under segue. I could have married Jena but then there was that bitch factor, Jena's father being the Mob boss not having a wife had spoiled his little girl beyond repair. Jena had a son with my Friend Joe. Joe is married to Deanne's first child, Wendy Michelle. We hadn't seen or heard from Jena in over two years.

We'd see Jack and Cindy often, Jack would come with their little girl and go out fishing with us. I'd see Dan, Shirley, and Maria whenever I visited Paxi. I missed Bob and even Montibelli. I was happy being with my family, but I was constantly checking the computer for something that could come up. My girls keep close eyes on me for me not to wander. I'm not a patient person, at least not when it comes to waiting for the next great adventure that I know is right around the next corner.